PENGUIN BOOKS

THE LAST STARSHIP FROM EARTH

John Boyd was born in 1919 and brought up in Atlanta, Georgia. He was commissioned into the U.S. Navy in 1940 and served in northern Russia, England, Japan, and the Philippines. He was the only junior officer mentioned in Samuel Eliot Morison's naval history of World War II. After Mr. Boyd's marriage in 1944 he finished his degree in history and journalism at the University of Southern California. He is the author of nearly a dozen science-fiction novels, including *The Pollinators of Eden, The Rakehells of Heaven* (both also published by Penguin Books), and, most recently, *The Girl with the Jade Green Eyes*. John Boyd lives with his wife in Los Angeles.

D1354249

The
Last Starship
from
Earth

By JOHN BOYD

PENGUIN BOOKS

Dedicated to the memory of
Henry Tudor VIII

Penguin Books Ltd, Harmondsworth,
Middlesex, England
Penguin Books, 625 Madison Avenue,
New York, New York 10022, U.S.A.
Penguin Books Australia Ltd, Ringwood,
Victoria, Australia
Penguin Books Canada Limited, 2801 John Street,
Markham, Ontario, Canada L3R 1B4
Penguin Books (N.Z.) Ltd, 182–190 Wairau Road,
Auckland 10, New Zealand

First published in the United States of America by
Weybright and Talley, Inc., 1968
First published in Canada by
Clarke, Irwin & Company Limited 1968
Published in Penguin Books 1978

LIBRARY OF CONGRESS CATALOGING IN PUBLICATION DATA
Upchurch, Boyd.
   The last starship from Earth.
   Reprint of the 1968 ed. published by Weybright
and Talley, New York.
I. Title.
[PZ4.U63Las 1978]   [PS3571.P35]
813'.5'4   77-26235
ISBN 0 14 00.4875 8

Printed in the United States of America by
Offset Paperback Mfrs., Inc., Dallas, Pennsylvania
Set in Times Roman

Preface to the Penguin Edition

THE FOLLOWING NOVEL IS ONE OF A TRILOGY BASED ON CLASSIC myths. Insofar as a writer plans for the marketing of his books, I chose mythic themes in hope of sounding echoes in the racial memory of readers. Such a scheme may sound a trifle grandiose, a form of Jungian commercialism, but it has a defensible rationale. As Carl Sagan implies, the eons-old reptilian complex of the human brain may retain neural patterns fixed on it by our terror of dinosaurs, our memory of dragons, which may well be the chthonic source of science fiction's bug-eyed monsters. Then, too, there was the realization that a story that survives for three thousand years must hold a permanent and compelling interest.

Such stories did for me, so I rewrote them in a futuristic setting, at times changing tragedy to comedy, and serious social comment to satire. Aficionados of science fiction know the pleasure of reading in the genre. There was also a great pleasure in writing these tales.

One of the problems in attempting to define science fiction is that the genre is too versatile, but its openness is a boon to writers. A free-form art in style and substance, the genre invites wanton wiles, requires little research, and is open to sly plagiarisms. Here, too, a writer may indulge his weakness for extravagant metaphors.

To the writer-reader, science fiction offers a fruited garden of varied delights landscaped around a promontory. Flash Gordon and Buck Rogers were successful science-fiction comic strips. *Rhodan* was a series of paperbacks with a comic-strip scenario, and *Star Wars* was an explosive success as a comic-strip movie. Atop the promontory stand the significant works of gifted and complex writers, the George Orwells and Aldous Huxleys. Perhaps on the lower slopes, still growing and waiting to be ranked, are the thought-provoking, futuristic adventures of an H. G. Wells or an Anthony Burgess and the latter-day mythos of J. R. R. Tolkien.

Stylistically, the genre ranges from the subaqueous and mystical Ray Bradbury to the elegantly mechanistic Arthur Clarke, who alone of us dares put reciprocating engines in fairyland, something in the garden for anyone with a taste for strange fruit.

My interest in science fiction evolved from a boyhood spent reading pulp magazines after being given impetus in the direction of science fiction by Jack London's *The Star Rover*. The interest took a long time to incubate into action. I was forty-seven before I submitted a science-fiction story for publication, and the idea for the story had germinated for almost twenty years.

Rarely does a writer know the day or the hour when a story idea comes to him, but the idea for my first story came between two and three o'clock on a Friday afternoon in late April, 1946. I was sitting in a sociology class at the University of Southern California, listening to the involved, obfuscating, and nonsubstantive jargon of the professor, when it struck me that the language of sociologists was a fitting subject for satire. At the moment I knew I had the subject for the story, if not the form.

A short time later, a story appeared in *The Saturday Evening Post* dealing with a theme close to an English major's heart, the fictional re-creation of the life and art of a blind Homer of the spaceways. The tale was Robert Heinlein's unforgettable, unforgotten "The Cool Green Hills of Earth," and I had found the form for my satire—futuristic.

Hoping for a maximum of money for a minimum of effort, I wrote the idea in the form of a radio drama slanted for the then popular *Skippy Theater*. The drama described a young man, Haldane, on trial for impregnating a girl outside his own profession in an overpopulated world where human beings were bred to serve the needs of the state. The judge and jury were sociologists, and Haldane's lawyer was faced with the task of interpreting his client's lucid and straightforward testimony into the involved syntax of sociologists in order to make Haldane's motives understood to the judge and jury.

I thought the finished play was the most scintillating bit of social comedy since Sheridan. Surprisingly, the producer of the radio show did not callously disagree. He sent a letter with the returned manuscript, expressing his regret that the play did not fit his show's format and asking me to submit more of my work. But the play, then called *The Fairweather Syndrome*, constituted my entire oeuvre. With it, I shot my wad.

I threw the manuscript away but could not rid myself of the idea. After I left school and went about earning a living, I added mystic dimensions to the plot, further complications, more humor and sadness. Not writing the story, merely toying with it as the concern over the population explosion made the central idea more germane, I decided to write a science-fiction epic along Miltonian lines which, instead of justifying the ways of God to man, would justify the ways of a god to a man. It's easy to write an epic in the imagination; working it out on paper is more difficult.

This was a time-track novel, however. It occupied a time parallel to, and at points coinciding with, our own times, but different. The hero was still Haldane, but now he was a mathematician who grew interested in literature. The device allowed me to rewrite and to revise famous poems at my pleasure and to quote great works from my memory without having to check the source.

One of the delights in writing the narrative came in the creation of two original poems that the plot demanded. Derivative from Yeats and Shelley, the poems, in my opinion, were well wrought, at least on a par with the middle works of Robert W. Service and Edgar Guest.

Finally, to rid myself of an incubus, I finished and typed the novel. Looking around for a title—I did not wish to call it *The Fairweather Syndrome* because "syndrome" was not a word of general currency—I spotted *The Last Train from Atlanta* on my library shelf and considered it a good omen, since Atlanta is my native town. I called my book *The Last Starship from Earth*. It was a happy theft because it was a title in line with a paradox in the story: My last starship had lifted off from Earth some time around 34 A.D. or 1968, depending on the time track. Heinlein liked the work well enough to endorse it, to my knowledge the first time he ever endorsed a novel, and it was fitting that he should, since his story had helped foster the tale.

The mythic connotations of man's fall from grace seemed to work with the first novel, so in planning the second I unabashedly borrowed the myth of Phaedra. The heroine was named Freda, and her younger, illicit lover, Hippolina. I culled one of the tale's climactic speeches almost intact from Racine's *Phèdre*, and why not? He took the idea from Euripides.

Here again I attempted to infuse the narrative with the poetic shimmerings of "The Cool Green Hills of Earth," but it is harder to write a poetic novel than to write a poetic short story. Sustaining a unified style for *The Pollinators of Eden* was made even more difficult by the fact that the last book I read before beginning the novel was Oriana Fallaci's *When the Sun Dies,* and her stylistic tricks kept popping up from my subconscious like plums from Jack Horner's pudding. So I used them, too.

In the classic myth, Phaedra, remorseful over her incestuousness, strangles herself. In creating Freda, the thinking man's ideal woman who could quote Shakespeare while making love, I grew so charmed by her I could not submit her to strangulation. In fact, I destroyed Hippolina to keep him from getting to her, so reluctant was I to let her submit to the caresses of another man. She was mine. John Wyndham solved the problem. When Freda finally yielded, it was to a lesbian orchid on a planet of ambulatory plants.

I loved the paradox in the title *The Pollinators of Eden.* Logically there could have been no pollinators in Eden. Once Adam and Eve discovered the process of reproduction, there was no longer an Eden. They were ejected for their "sin."

If the books in this trilogy were characters from Shakespeare, *The Rakehells of Heaven* would have to be Edmund from *King Lear.* It was a whoreson of science fiction, but there was great sport in its making.

Initially the story was based on the myth of Prometheus, but my hero was to bring to men not fire but the truth of their origins, as XYY chromosome-bearers who were cast out of Heaven. Following the classical pattern, my Prometheus was to be torn by the Furies at the denouement, but strange things happened on the way to the denouement.

Two space scouts from Imperial Earth land on a planet that might have been the native home of mankind and the origin of man's concept of Heaven. The scouts, an atavistic Southern Baptist and an atavistic Irish Catholic, find themselves appalled at the tolerance and permissiveness of the nearly human society they find on the planet and set out to institute a more rigid system of morality and ethics among the beings. Conflict develops between the Earth men over the form the "conversion" is to take.

The story was told from the viewpoint of the Southerner, a Junior Johnson of the spaceways, and in the vernacular of the "good old boy." As the plot developed and the characters emerged, my sympathies shifted from the Southerner to the Irish con artist, and I found the style, "Southern rhodomontade," a sheer delight.

At times I would awaken my wife in the wee hours of the morning, chuckling over some riposte between the characters.

Gradually the mythic overtones of the story faded, and the Irishman won first place in my affections. He remains in Heaven— a self-convert to Judaism, apparently—while the Southerner, believing himself a murderer, is exiled back to Earth. Ramming his starship back through space, he attempts to exceed the speed of light, prove the Grandfather paradox, and abort the mission before it starts; and he fails, by a space of a few days, but it's a wild ride he takes.

Again on Earth, he is torn by inner Furies. No one will accept his revelations because it is obvious that he is a Jesus freak who has gone around the bend.

The ideal reader of *The Rakehells of Heaven* should have the mentality of a Southern stock-car racer, be a Baptist with a sense of detachment, have a well-developed sense of the absurd, and be fascinated with the quirks and accomplishments of the human animal. One ideal reader was the writer, who enjoyed every page of the manuscript.

J. B.
1978

ix

Though fondly we hope and fervently pray that this great scourge of war shall speedily pass, still we must not derogate the promise of the laser science so misused by the lesser angels of our nature.

Acceleration of light quanta, while sweeping aside old boundaries of physical science, issues grave warnings to the social sciences. We may yet disenthrall ourselves from history to become the judges of our own past — gods of ourselves, as it were.

Let us then so conduct ourselves in the right, as we are given to see the right, that these generations shall not vanish from the annals of time.

A. LINCOLN

Chapter One

RARELY IS IT GIVEN MAN TO KNOW THE DAY OR THE HOUR when fate intervenes in his destiny, but, because he had checked his watch just before he saw the girl with the hips, Haldane IV knew the day, the hour, and the minute. At Point Sur, California, on September 5, at two minutes past two, he took the wrong turn and drove down a lane to hell.

Ironically, he was following his roommate's directions, and if there was one thing he had learned in two years at Berkeley, it was that students of theological cybernetics didn't know right from left. He was driving down to see a working model of a laser propulsion pod, and Malcolm had told him that the science museum was off the road to the right, across from the art gallery. He turned right and found himself in the parking area for the art gallery, across the road from the science museum.

Self-respecting students of mathematics rarely visited art galleries: but there it beckoned, its entrance esplanade curving up from the parking lot to a point of rock where the building, reminding him of a gull launching itself into flight, was cantilevered over the Pacific two hundred feet below.

It was a pleasant day. A breeze standing in from the ocean tempered the sunlight. The verandah of the building commanded a wide view of the ocean to the northwest. He looked at his watch and decided he had time to spare.

He had parked his car and headed toward the entrance when he saw the girl ahead of him. Her stride was long, and her hips swayed slightly with each step as if her pelvis were a cam which created an interesting moment of force around its axis. It was several microseconds before the

1

aesthetics of her motion intruded on his consideration of its mathematics. Proletarian girls used such a sway as a lure, but this girl wore the tunic and pleated skirt of a professional.

He slowed to keep a few paces behind her as she passed through the entrance into the rotunda and stopped to look at a painting. Anxious for a view of her frontal geometry, Haldane walked up beside her and, as she studied the painting, inspected her unobtrusively. He saw chestnut hair gleaming with highlights, a firm but rounded chin, eyebrows arched in a clean line above hazel eyes, a long neck, high, erect breasts, and a flat stomach planing into the long V of her thighs.

She turned, suddenly, and caught his gaze. Feigning a questioning look, he threw his hand toward the painting. "What is it?"

In the manner of the professional, she looked through him, not at him, as she answered, "It depicts motion."

He threw what he hoped was a practiced glance toward the canvas and said, "Well, the lines seem to move."

Her words were stamped from her lips. "It spins. It upsets my stomach."

He glanced down at the A–7 stenciled on her tunic. The A meant that she was a student artist, but he did not know what subclass seven meant—possibly that of art critic. "I've heard that tea is a remedy for nausea. May I treat you to a cup of first aid?"

Her face was still impassive, but her eyes were focused on his. "Do you usually accost females in art galleries?"

"Ordinarily I work the churches, but today is Saturday."

The eyes were laughing from the mask. "You may buy me a cup of tea if you wish to waste credits on an extracategorical virgin."

"Saturday's my day for virgins."

He led her onto the verandah and chose a table close to the railing from which they could look directly down on the surf at the base of the cliff. As he seated her and snapped his fingers for the waitress, he said, "I'm Haldane IV, M–5, 138270, 3/10/46."

"Helix, A–7, 148361, 13/15/47."

"From the minute I spoke to you, I figured you were Swedish, but what does the seven mean?"

"Poetry."

"You're the first in that category I've ever met."

"There aren't many of us," she said, as the waitress rolled a tray to the table. "Sugar and cream?"

"One lump, please, and a dash of cream. . . . It's tragic that there aren't more of you," he said, admiring the fluid harmony of her arm and wrist motion as she dropped his lumps.

"How gracious of a mathematician to speak thus of poetry."

"I wasn't talking about that stuff. I was just regretting that you've got such a narrow selection of mates to elect from. You'll probably end up with some lank-haired boy bard who'll leave you alone in the meadow while he wanders off to declaim to some scraggly buttercup."

"Citizen, you are atavistic," she reproached him, and her voice dropped an octave. "But I'm sympathetic to primitive emotions. My specialty is eighteenth-century romantic poetry. . . . Did you know that before the Starvation there was a cult of inseminators called 'lovers' and that one of the greatest of them all was a poet, Lord Byron."

"I'll have to look him up."

"Don't let your mother catch you reading him."

"She couldn't. She's dead, from an accidental fall."

"Oh, I'm sorry. I'm fortunate. I have foster parents, but both are alive and they dote on me. My parents were killed in a rocket crash. . . .

"But you amaze me that you know so little about my category. One of your big mathematicians, an M–5 if I remember correctly, wrote poetry which I never cared for but the intelligentsia seem to read. Perhaps you've heard of Fairweather I, the man who designed the pope?"

"Citizen, are you trying to tell me that Fairweather I wrote that . . . poetry?" He looked at her with genuine amazement.

"Don't be so shocked, Haldane. After all, diddling with ditties is not dalliance with a damsel."

Now he was shocked, horrified, and pleased. He wasn't

3

sure of the word "damsel" but he could interpolate, and he knew that for the first time in his life he had heard a female originate a witty remark. Moreover, it was the first time in his life he had ever heard a female professional not in a house of recreation volunteer so titillating a witticism from behind such a titivating façade.

In this girl, he had found the square root of minus one.

"I've got a right to be shocked," he said, hiding his immediate confusion behind a deeper-seated confusion. "My field is Fairweathian mathematics. I've studied the man ever since I was in grammar school. I came down here today to look at a model of a laser pod he invented in that museum across the road. I know he had the most inventive mind that ever existed, with the exception of yours and mine, but not a one of my professors, not a teacher, not a fellow student, nor even my father ever mentioned that he wrote a line of poetry. Up until right now, I thought I was the most unauthoritative expert in the world on Fairweather I, so you will pardon me if I seem a little groggy."

"I'm sure that no one was trying to keep it a secret from you," she said. "Perhaps none of your professors know it. Perhaps they are ashamed of it, and in this instance, I think, they would have a right to be."

"Why so?"

"I'm happy your man succeeded in mathematics, and I know he did quite well in theology, but in my opinion he failed miserably as a poet."

"Helix, you're a smart girl. I wouldn't think of disputing your knowledge in your field, but anything that man did, he must have done superbly. I wouldn't know an anapest from an antipasto, but if he wrote it, it was good."

"Proof of the pile is in the protons," she said. "I have a photographic memory, and the only thing he ever wrote that I can quote are lines a very old man told me when I was a little girl, and they were told in the context of a curiosity rather than as a poem."

"Recite it for me." He was suddenly interested.

"The title's almost as long as the poem," she said. "He

4

called it 'Reflections from a Higher Place, Revised.' It goes:

> Since you are tortured on a rack of time compressing,
> I'll murder you, beloved, as my final blessing.
> > You grew too old too young.
> > Speech has stilled your tongue.
> Summoning all my social grace
> I mix the hemlock to your taste.
>
> He told us from another place
> That he who loses wins the race,
> That parallel lines all meet in space.
> Yet, love, I'll mourn your angry face.

She moued disapproval. "He dotes on those silly little paradoxes such as racks compressing and blessing with murder. It's all sheer nonsense."

Haldane thought for a moment. "It sounds like he's rephrasing the Sermon on the Mount modified by Einstein's General Theory. 'He who loses wins the race' is another way of saying 'The meek shall inherit the earth.' That would explain the title, too. The 'higher place' is the Mount, and the reflections were 'revised' by Einstein."

She looked at him with amazement and admiration. "Why, Haldane IV, you're a Neanderthal genius! You're right, I'm sure. Neither the old man nor I ever thought of that, and your interpretation would account for the living dead."

Now he was amazed. "Who are the living dead?"

"Oh, you know, the Hell exiles, the official corpses."

Her answer brought him back to earth. "What have they got to do with it?"

"The old man, a blood relative of mine, used to know one of those Gray Brothers who put the exiles on the Hell ships. This was back in the days when they walked aboard, and this monk was saying he was having a rough time because halfway up the gangplank a female felon got hysterical—who wouldn't?—and started to scream and fight.

"The monks were getting the worst of it when some man up ahead in the line shouted back, 'He who loses wins the race, and parallel lines all meet in space.'

5

"When the man said that, she quieted down and went aboard as if she were taking a solar-system ship to another planet. . . . I see, now, that he was giving her religious consolation in shorthand.

"Still, I prefer Shelley. Have you read his 'Ode to the South Wind'?"

Haldane listened, but a part of his mind kept returning to Fairweather's subversive hobby. Every man to his own avocation, but it was ironical that the poem which braced the exiles was written by the man who had invented the propulsion system which hurled them to the frozen planet called Hell, discovered by Fairweather's probes and named by Fairweather, obviously just as he felt a paradox coming on.

Helix was a freshman at Golden Gate University and planned to teach in her category. She was eager to discuss her field of study, and her interest carried him along with her. Lovelace and Herrick, Suckling and Donne, Keats, Shelley, the archaic names came as easily to her tongue as the names of friends, and she quoted them in mirth or nostalgia. Her voice sounding above the surge of the surf wove around him a feeling for golden beginnings, and he was touched by a sense of history.

Finally the slanting sunlight carving shadows on the mountains westward aroused them to the knowledge that they must go.

She walked ahead of him across the verandah, and watching her walk, he called, "What was that one about the sceptered race?"

> "Ah, what avails the sceptred race,
>   Ah, what the form divine,
> What every virtue, every grace?
>   Rose Harmon, all were thine."

"That's you, Helix," he shouted with gusto, "from back here."

"Hush, you silly nut! Someone might hear you."

He walked with her to her car and held the door for her. "Haldane, you have the gallantry of Sir Lancelot."

6

"You didn't tell me about him. Would you be brave enough to meet me some evening in San Francisco, like tomorrow night, and tell me about this Sir Lancelot in some appropriate setting, say the tap room of the Sir Francis Drake?"

"How do you know I'm not a policewoman?"

"How do you know I'm not a policeman?"

"I was thinking of your safety," she smiled. "I can take care of policemen."

With a wave of her hand, she was gone.

He walked slowly back to his car, thinking that there must be something wrong with his body chemistry. He had sat and talked for a while with a girl who was swallowed, forever, by the vast anonymity of San Francisco; yet he had been happy in her presence, and now he was sad.

He drove his car onto the highway and engaged its pilot with the Berkeley band, enjoying the surge of power that told him the road was clear for miles ahead. Leaning back as he flicked along between gray mountains and the blue sea, he indulged in a rare moment of introspection.

Somewhere in the matrix of humanity eastward, where even the crags of the Rockies housed the abodes of human beings, there was a girl of eighteen who would be chosen for him by geneticists. She would be shock-haired and square-jawed, no doubt, as were most female mathematicians. Witty she might be, and kind, fully worthy of all devotion, but from this point onward she would have one drawback—she would not be Helix of the Golden Gate.

As the car dipped into a grove and the long shadows of the redwoods flicked their latticework beneath him, Haldane savored the bittersweetness of farewell. He was twenty, and it was twilight, and he had said 'good-by' forever to a girl who had come to him as a Deirdre had come to Irishmen of old, in such beauty and with such grace that flowers had leaned toward her as she walked. Then she had left him, and the winds of September rustling past his speeding car sang ballads of times when men had walked the earth as kings, of times three hundred years removed from this year of Our Lord. . . . His red warning light snapped him out of the reverie.

7

They were always working on those magnetic bands, tearing them out and laying them back in. Well, he consoled himself, as he took the wheel for manual steering, he could use a little exercise.

When Haldane entered the room he shared with Malcolm VI, his roommate was working at his desk with a row of figures projecting a probability curve for the occurrence of blue-beaked parakeets over a given number of generations and commencing with a given number of progenitors.

"Hey, Malcolm, guess what!"

"What?"

"I met a lady on Point Sur, full beautiful, a fairie child. Her stride was long, and her eyes were bright, and her words were wild. She was a poet. Ever meet that category?"

"There's a clutch of them over at the Golden Gate. Fell in with a brood, once, whilst on a mild drunk along the Barbary Coast. Listening to their talk is quaffing beakers of moonshine. By the holy feedback, they're weird sisters, pale brothers, all."

"This one was vive la different."

Haldane threw himself on his bunk, rolled to his back, and cupped his head in his clasped palms. "Yea, holy brother, her field is primitive poetry, and she's picked up a lot of information that wasn't in that history book I read.

"When she quotes that love poetry, you can hear the old dulcimers melting them pleasure domes of ice, and damsels start wailing for demon lovers."

"Sounds like she's doing research for Belle's Place."

"With her, it's antiquarianism, so it's legal. Say, did you know our boy, Fairweather, wrote a poem?"

"Do you jest?"

"I jest not."

"By the overheated tubes of the pope, Haldane, I think you're touched. You'd better take a quick trip down to Belle's and purge yourself of subversive thoughts. Besides, I'm in need of assistance."

"You still on that chromosome chart?"

8

"Yes."

Haldane rose, walked over, and looked down at the equations Malcolm had scrawled beside the chart and then at the chart. Various lines of symbols diverged from a base, and at intervals along the lines a blue X marked the occurrence of blue-beaked parakeets. A few of the symbols were circled with O and the line stopped.

In Denver, Washington, Atlanta, geneticists worked over such charts, but for a far different purpose than that inherent in Malcolm's exercise. Once Haldane had taken an elective in genetics and had seen the human charts on professional dynasties. Occasionally there would be blank areas where no births occurred, and, infrequently, the blank areas followed a red X with the notation $S.O.S.$— Sterilized by Order of the State.

Looking down at Malcolm's chart, Haldane did not think of these things, but they were a part of his memory. What he thought, he voiced. "Talk about poets talking moonshine! You've been given a problem with the answer inherent in the proposition. Don't figure it step by step. Just solve for the blue X, and let the rest follow. . . . this way. . . ."

"But I'm supposed to kill off random samplings of parakeets, at least one dead for every twenty. What happens if an eagle swoops down and eats this parakeet here?"

"That's your choice. You're the eagle. But remember, a blank means a crumpled little mass of feathers that will wing no more through the golden sunlight."

Malcolm looked up at his roommate. "You'd better go down there, boy. One afternoon with a poet and you have subconsciously considered dalliance outside your category which is miscegenation; you've implicitly questioned the policies of the state, which is deviationism; and you've made light of your own profession which reflects on your *esprit de corps*."

"Instead of advice," Haldane suggested, "why don't you put your talents to figuring the statistical possibilities of two persons meeting twice by accident in a city of eight million people?"

"Take your problems to the pope."

9

"What a wonderful world you live in, Malcolm, where every problem can be solved by the pope or a prostitute."

Malcolm jutted his second finger up from his palm.

Haldane walked out onto the balcony and looked across the bay where the glow of San Francisco was growing brighter in the deepening dusk. Mentally he lined his sight on the campus of Golden Gate University.

She would be at her desk now, in her dormitory room, bent over a book, her left arm crooked around it, and the light from her desk lamp would glow on the down of her arms. She would have been to the shower and be clean-smelling of soap with the highlights glinting in her hair.

Suddenly it occurred to Haldane that he was thinking in imagery. No doubt poets thought like this, because, for a moment, more than his brain had been involved. For a moment he had smelled the fragrance of her hair, and he had felt again that peculiar upsurge of pleasure which he had gained from her company.

Helix would be happy to know that he could think like a poet, but she never would know.

If he wished, he could pull his telephone from his pocket, dial her genetic number, and bounce his words and image directly to her. He even had a reason for calling, to check the Dewey decimal reference to a volume by Sir Lancelot.

Her answer would come in precise, measured tones giving him the number and a choice of titles. And that would be the end of Haldane IV, for sure.

She would know beyond cavil that his question was a blind thrown over his primitive yearnings, for that girl studied atavism as a prerequisite to Limerick-writing I.

A casual conversation with a boy on a sunny afternoon was no more than a slight pleasantry, but a second conversation, deliberately sought, would indicate danger. Their meeting would have to seem an accident so natural that her defenses would not be alerted.

He did not know at what point his thoughts resolved into a decision, but he knew that he had made it, despite the peril. The reward was worth the risk.

Out across the bay a sprite of a lass was poring over

10

tomes of old romance. He would cloak his eighteenth-century romanticism under a patina of twentieth-century social realism and come a-calling. He might have to memorize a few poems to create the right atmosphere, but with his memory it should be no problem. Little did the lass know that soon, very soon, romance would be incarnate in her life, that the gossamer, many-hued fabric of her dreaming would be given solid substance by the magic wand of Haldane IV.

At Berkeley, four years before, a student professional in mathematics had brought about the ruin of a home economics major. Both had been S.O.S. ed and declassed, and the mathematician had gone on to become famous as a quarterback for the Forty-niners. In campus slang, it would never be said of Haldane IV that he was "quarterbacking for the Forty-niners." But there was a risk, and standing on the balcony, he accepted it.

As a whisper in his memory, lines she had quoted came back to him, and he voiced them, slightly altered, into the deepening night.

> The church and state can go to hell
> And I'll go to my Helix.

Chapter Two

DURING THE FOLLOWING SCHOOL WEEK, HALDANE PLOTted his second meeting with the girl on graph paper, using only variables, and he cursed a field of study which led a student to art lectures, concerts, recitals, and museums, and into low cafés and bars in San Francisco. Where to search was the easiest of his three problems, but surveying that one area convinced him that people were taking this art stuff too seriously.

Because the Golden Gate University was there, his base of operations would have to be in San Francisco. That meant he would have to work out of the ancestral apartment, because he couldn't afford to rent a room for weekends without asking his father for help. His father presented problems enough as it was: the old man was a member of the Department of Mathematics, as such he was an officer of the state, and his natural, unaroused suspicions would demand a verbal adroitness from Haldane easily equal to his mathematical talents.

He would need a solid reason to explain his association with art students to his father and his friends.

Science majors regarded the arty crowd as strictly back-of-the-bus society. Writers flaunted tams, painters wore tunics an inch longer than standard, and the musicians never moved their lips when they talked. All of them affected long-handled, water-cooled cigarette holders, and when they smoked they flicked ashes with a swish. Despite public acceptance of their product, they were socially relegated to a few cheap bars and cafés around San Francisco, to Southern California, and to France.

No mathematician would sully his thinking with the privately defined symbols they used in conversations which were designed not for communication but for "expression." In his brief encounters with those people, Haldane had never before in the history of his social relations heard so many say so much about so little.

Personally, he tolerated them as long as they kept in their place. Their lank-haired frails slunk along instead of walking and were, with the overpowering exception of Helix, as hipless as the males were shoulderless.

Haldane avoided making generalities about groups, but generalities could be made: colored peoples were usually colored, Fiji Islanders ate less blubber than Eskimos, and mathematicians were more precise thinkers than artists.

Yet, his feelings toward them were not entirely condemnatory. They testified to the variety and versatility of life forms on the planet, and as such they were a tribute to the magnanimity of the Creator.

Haldane's father, a statistician, was not so liberal. In fact, he was bigoted. He felt that all nonmathematicians were second-class citizens, and he refused to integrate. His attitude amused Haldane, a theoretical mathematician who considered statisticians on a par with hod-carriers, but this statistician was a department member whose spoken command had the force of law. He would be perturbed by his son's attending art lectures. His perturbation would be *in extremis* if he suspected his son intended to commit miscegenation, and with an art female.

Sooner or later, Haldane would have to give *the* reason. The old man was inquisitive, argumentative, and dictatorial. Worse, he was an inveterate chess player. Haldane had begun to beat him consistently when he was sixteen, and the psychic trauma resulting had left his father convinced that his defeats—and he lost ninety per cent of the time—were flukes.

Haldane III would hardly be impressed by his son's presence on week-ends; he would be suspicious. Haldane averaged a week-end a month at home, and some months he forgot. His attitude toward his father had always been one of detached affection that was more affectionate the more detached it was.

Then, his meeting with the girl after he found her would have to be casual and easily explained. If she suspected him, she would be off like a starship in overdrive. After ingratiating himself, he would need a room to take her to in a most casual and logical manner without seeming to lure her. Thereafter, the Haldane charm would become the vehicle of dalliance.

Luck guided him to a trysting place.

Malcolm's parents owned an apartment in San Francisco. They had left four months ago for a year's trip to New Zealand to teach Maori priests theological cybernetics for their papal communiqués. Haldane knew about the apartment, for Malcolm went over occasionally to check it and dust the furniture. Haldane would have never taken his roommate into his confidence and asked for the key. Basically, he didn't trust Malcolm. Malcolm didn't smoke, drank very little, and went to church regularly.

On Thursday, Malcolm entered the room waving a paper. "Haldane, I have failed to flunk. Thank you, mattress master."

Haldane, from flat on his back, recognized the chart on

blue-beaked parakeets and could see it was marked with a $B+$.

He was irked. "Why was it marked down from A?"

"The prof graded it and penalized me for lack of neatness."

"He shouldn't use subjective criteria for an objective test."

"He figured it was subjective, since I was the eagle, so he didn't run it through the grading machine. . . . When I ate the parakeet, some of the feathers dropped on my plate."

Out of the talent of Haldane, sired by his long contemplation, the colt of inspiration was foaled at a full gallop.

"You know, Malcolm, if Fairweather I could reduce moral laws to mathematical equivalents and store them in a memory bank to create the pope, why couldn't I break down the components of a sentence, give each unit a mathematical weight, and design a machine for scanning and grading written essays?"

Malcolm thought a moment.

"For you, I think it would be a simple task except for two reasons: you're not a grammarian, and you're not Fairweather."

"Yes, and I don't know anything about literature, but I read fast."

"What you propose is beyond the limit of things ascertainable. If I recall correctly, and I don't have a photographic memory, Fairweather I had 312 gradations of the meaning of a single term, murder, ranging all the way from murder for profit to state euthanasia for undesirable proletarians. You would have to analyze every figure of speech in the language."

"He didn't analyze every gradation," Haldane objected. "He took two extremes and worked toward the middle."

"I wouldn't know that."

"Listen, this idea might be a contribution!" He got up and paced the room, partly for dramatic affect and partly from genuine enthusiasm. "I can see the title page of the publication, now. There it is, in 14-point Bodoni bold: A

14

MATHEMATICAL EVALUATION OF AESTHETIC FACTORS IN LITERATURE, by Haldane IV. . . . No, I'll use Garamond."

He wheeled and pounded his fist into his palm. "Think what this could mean. Literature professors wouldn't have to grade essays, just stick them in the old slot."

Malcolm, seated on the edge of his bed, looked up at Haldane with genuine concern. "Haldane, there's something frightening about you. A vagrant thought passes your mind, and, wham, it's an obsession.

"By the infallible transistors of the pope, I swear you're touched with madness. Methinks you'd disinter the bones of Shakespeare, reflesh them once again, and lead them through a new quadrille."

Haldane was impressed by his name dropping. "You seem to know something about literature yourself."

"Indeed. My mother was the seventh daughter of the seventh daughter of a minnesinger. I wanted to be a wandering minstrel, but my father was a mathematician."

"If I follow this idea up," Haldane said, as if he were concentrating aloud, "I'll have to spend my week-ends in San Francisco, at literary lectures. Dad will be a problem with his chess games. If only I had a place to be alone for a few hours."

"You could use Ma and Pa's apartment, if you'd dust it."

"Dust it! I'd mop it."

"It mops itself. It's the *objets d'art* in the living room that the carriers of my genes wish protected."

He walked over to his desk, pulled out a key, and handed it to Haldane who took it with feigned casualness.

Haldane III was grudgingly pleased that his son had decided to come home for week-ends. In the beginning, he asked no questions and Haldane volunteered no information. Sooner or later, the questions would come, Haldane knew, and it would make his actions seem more authentic if his father had to wheedle the information out of him.

He visited the quarters of Malcolm's parents, a four-room apartment eight floors up with a view of the bay, and he memorized the movable contents of the living room using a crude mnemonics system. If the brocaded tiger on the backrest of the divan were to lunge three feet forward, it would strike the nose of an elongated roebuck, a lamp base, carved from wood.

With heavy furniture he did not concern himself. A policeman planting a microphone in the room wouldn't take the effort to move it.

He thought the apartment ornate, but the view of the bay from its wide front window compensated for its flamboyance. After he completed his check, he stood idly gazing out on Alcatraz and the hills beyond when a line from something she had said popped into his mind: "What mad pursuit? What pipes and timbrels?"

A very good question. What mad pursuit had led him here? What mystic pipes and timbrels had he heard to lure him on? It was not normal for a worldly lad of twenty to make such elaborate plans to experience what could only be a minor variation, at best, on an old and familiar theme.

Then the image of the girl's face returned to his memory and he saw, again, the shadow of sadness behind the laughter in her eyes, heard her voice weaving around him the charms which had enchained him with their visions of other worlds and other times. Her memory triggered anew that chemical reaction in the blood which had confounded him, and he knew what pipes were calling. . . . He heard, and he would follow, tripping lightly on his goat hoofs, the irresistible keening of the pipes of Pan.

Two sorties the first week-end, a lecture on modern art at the civic center and a students' presentation of *Oedipus Rex* on the Golden Gate campus, produced only three typical A–7s. He was not disappointed. He was merely sniffing around to pick up the scent and not expecting to break the law of averages.

Back on campus, he squeezed every minute from his schedule to spend in the library reading the poetry and prose of the eighteenth century. He read rapidly with pinpoint concentration. Concepts fecundated in his mind like larvae in a fen, and one of the concepts on the periphery of his mire was the fear that he had undertaken to level Mount Everest with a spade.

John Keats died at 26, and that was the happiest event that ever occurred in the life of Haldane IV. If the poet had lived five more years, his works and the works written about his works would have meant two more libraries for Haldane to plow through.

To confound his confusion, he could not distinguish between the major works of minor poets and the minor works of major poets. As a result, he became the only undergraduate, internationally, who could quote long passages from Robert Browning's *The Ring and the Book*. Unknowingly, he was the world's exclusive authority on the works of Winthrop Mackworth Praed. He had Felicia Dorothea Hemans down cold.

Long hours of boredom were relieved by minutes of hair-pulling as he attempted to grasp hidden meanings behind curtains of unintelligible phrases.

In San Francisco, he was equally frustrated. Week moved into week with no trace of the girl. His father, who eventually wheedled from him his cover story, so little respected his son's activities that he resented their incursions into his chess games.

After six weeks, Haldane no longer needed the vision of that unworldly beauty to spur him on. He had become intrigued by the girl's ability to break the law of averages. She was performing statistical legerdemain.

On campus, he tore great chunks from the body of English Lit. with a monomania which deprived him of workouts at the gym, social intercourse with students, or dalliance at Belle's Place. Volume after volume fell behind him as husks behind the champion at a corn-husking. Librarians came to hold him in such awe that they gave him the private cubicle of a professor on sabbatical lest the rustle of paper by other students distract his fantastic concentration.

Finally, sodden with Shelley, Keats, Byron, Wordsworth, and Coleridge, with Felicia Dorothea Hemans oozing out of his pores, he collapsed across December 31, 1799, a long-distance runner making his final lunge at the tape. It was mid-afternoon on Friday when he closed his last book and stumbled out of the library into the wan sunlight of November.

He was vaguely surprised that it was November. October was his favorite month. Somewhere between Byron and Coleridge, he had lost October.

Bone tired, he drove home with a body that begged for rest, but the brain had scheduled a student concert at Golden Gate, and the body yielded. After checking 562 type A students, he found no Helix, but he stayed for the concert because his knowledge of music was weak. He discovered that Bach was somewhat easier to sleep by than Mozart.

On Saturday afternoon, he beat his father swiftly in three straight games of chess. During the fourth game, which the old man had acrimoniously insisted on and which Haldane had to win rapidly in order to get to a chamber-music recital he had planned, Haldane III looked up at his son and said, "How are your grades coming at school?"

"I'm still in the upper ten percent."

"You don't work at it."

"I don't have to. I inherited a splendid mind."

"You'd better start thinking about applying it. Mathematics is a broad field, and to get across it you have to work fast."

Haldane could sense a lecture paragraphs away, and he didn't particularly care for parental advice, particularly not in his present state of mental fatigue. Deliberately, he diverted the lecture by inviting an argument. "I don't think the field's so broad."

"My god, what arrogance!"

"I don't, Dad. Fairweather made the ultimate break-through when he jumped the time warp; mathematicians have merely been polishing the pieces. I'll prophesy that the next breakthrough in human progress will be by the psychologists."

Lightning flickered in the old man's eyes. "Psychologists! They don't even work with measurable phenomena."

Without being aware of his destination, Haldane launched himself into a sea of theory.

18

"It's not always the measurable phenomena that counts. From the point of view of their literature, our ancestors seem to have done nothing but fight; yet they had something we have lost, the spirit to operate as individuals. They went out and met challenges without relying on directives from sixteen different committees. That aynrandistic independence of action was smothered under the Dewey-influenced reign of Soc Henry VIII, that antihomopapal, mechanodeistic, category-beheader!"

"If you're deriding a state hero, watch your language, boy!"

"O.K., I withdraw the nominative modifiers. But, face it, Dad. On this best of all possible planets with the best of all possible social systems, we have nowhere to go but inward, and any renaissance of spirit will be an implosion triggered under the jurisdiction of the Department of Psychology."

Haldane III, the chess game forgotten, roared into battle.

"I tell you, you would-be grammarian, if the Department of Psychology ever develops anything, it'll be through an implant from the Department of Mathematics. Fairweather didn't know cold on Hell about theology, but he moved into Church and built a truly infallible pope which put an end to mealymouthed bulls and submontane temporizing."

"Yes, look at Fairweather," Haldane counterattacked. "He gave us the starships, and what happened? A few ships lost on the first probes, or maybe they just kept going, a few crewmen returning with space madness, and the triumvirate calls off the probes. We're socked in by Soc and psyched out by Psych!

"Where are those ships today? Two left, with their skeleton crews, and both are Hell ships. We've got the stars, and we haven't got the guts to unwrap the package. Now, what contributions can a mathematician make?"

Taken aback by the explosive sincerity of his son, Haldane III dropped to a key of disgruntled sarcasm. "If you spent half as much time in the lab as you do in those art palaces, you might be able to make some contribution

19

other than that inane sedimentation theory which should never have been accepted."

Gently, Haldane asked, "Dad, did you have a contribution on your record before you were twenty?"

"You whelp," his father said, paternal pride diluting his anger, "I've forgotten more math than you'll ever know. Your move."

Haldane glanced at his watch. Time was running short. He had to get ready for the recital, so he beat his father in four moves.

"Want to play another?" Haldane III asked. "We could make a little bet on the side."

Their side bets were drinks, with the loser mixing and serving.

"Nothing doing, dad. I'm a chess player, not a sadist. But I'll mix you one."

It was more than a drink, it was a peace offering, and his father accepted it.

As Haldane mixed the drink, his father, who was storing the chess pieces, said to him, "Talking about Fairweather I, Greystone's coming out next Saturday to lecture on the Fairweather Effect at the Civic Auditorium. Want to come along?"

"Sounds interesting," Haldane said, squeezing a lime.

It *was* interesting. Greystone was Secretary of the Department of Mathematics and was reputedly one of the few mathematicians who understood the Simultaneity Theorem on which the starships operated. Also, he had a genius for simplifying concepts.

"I might go along."

"This is not for publication, but I called Washington, yesterday, and talked to Greystone. He thinks he can get the alternate navigator for the "Styx" and the "Charon" to come along with him."

Haldane set the drink on the table in front of his father and said, "If he can get one of those surly freaks to say anything, it'll be a wonder."

"Greystone can if anyone can."

Despite his conventional remark about the spaceman, Haldane had a secret respect for the breed. From the original crews that manned the space probes over a hundred years ago, those who survived were the toughest of the tough.

On television he had often watched them arrive on the prison ships from Hell, surly, taciturn, the closest thing on earth to immortals because they aged only a few months, earth time, in each century. Broad-shouldered, heavy, more solidly built than their descendants, they were held to earth less by their own desire, Haldane sensed, than by the umbilical cord of their supply line.

"I'd like to go to the lecture," Haldane said, "if something more important doesn't come up."

"What could be more important than a lecture by Greystone on Fairweather I?"

"Look, dad," Haldane laid a casual arm across his father's shoulder, "if you want me to go along as an interpreter, then say so. But I tell you now that understanding Fairweather is less a matter of knowledge than of intuition."

"Instruct me, expert!"

Haldane went to the chamber-music recital that evening without much hope of seeing Helix, and he didn't. From the primitive jam session he drove to a coffee house which poets frequented, the Mermaid Tavern.

There were a few A–7 students present, and he fell in with them. His coat concealed his tunic, and in the dim glow of the table lamps they mistook him for one of them. One mentioned Browning, and he awed them by quoting at length from *The Ring and the Book*.

With their hands moving to accent their words, twisting their torsos forward to listen, squirming upright or sideways in affirmation or rebuttal, they reminded him of silverfish slithering around in some damp, dark corner. Yet their enthusiasm for a remembered phrase, quoted at times in the language of the writer, struck him with an impact similar to that he remembered when he had sat with Helix at Point Sur.

His disguise was ripped when one of them asked what he thought of the latest translation of Maria Rilke from the German.

With a fluting intonation, he answered, "I adore her in German, but Maria, in English, is blah!"

21

His questioner turned to a companion. "Did you hear the man, Philip? He adores *her* in German."

"What are you, fellow? A police pigeon?"

"Maybe he's a soc major out researching the peasantry."

Haldane dropped the fluting, "When you call me a sociologist, boy bard, smile!"

"Move it, fellow, before we move it for you."

He could have taken any three of them at one time, but there were five of them. He moved it. He didn't want a dean's reprimand at this stage.

Driving back to Berkeley, he was perplexed. In his two and a half months of searching for Helix, he had visited and revisited the places where she should have been. Many of the A–7 students he had seen several times, but there was no Helix. Something had gone wrong with the laws of probability.

He did not go to the Fairweather lecture.

On Wednesday, he was dining in the student union when he saw a notice in the school paper. A Professor Moran was giving a lecture on the Golden Gate campus Friday evening on eighteenth-century romantic poetry. When he saw the item, he couldn't finish his meal, but got up and walked out. If Helix didn't go to this lecture, she'd never go to another on this earth.

On his way home he realized he had a weakness which could betray him—his nerves. He had geared himself to such a high pitch of expectancy that he might break.

He could see himself meeting her. But instead of a look of pleased surprise spreading over his face, he fell to the floor and crawled toward her, clutching her ankles and moaning hysterically in his relief and joy.

Regally she gazed down on the fallen lad in shock and disdain, kicked her ankles free, and walked over and away from him, forever.

He smiled at his own imagery as he climbed the stairs, but an insight gave his thoughts a graver tone. His immersion into literature had given an emotional cast and color to his thoughts. Strangely, the world seemed more vivid.

Haldane's father was disappointed when Haldane told him that he could not go with him to the Greystone lecture. Seeing the disappointment on his father's face, Haldane felt remorse.

"I'm sorry, Dad, but I can't bring myself to miss the lecture on the romantic period. It falls exactly into the time period I've chosen to demonstrate my mathematical analysis of literary styles. Anyway, the Fairweather lecture is too advanced for a sophomore. In my sixth year, I'll be up to my ears in Fairweather Mechanics, and if you can pick up a transcript of the lecture for my reserve notes, I'd appreciate it. This poetry reading has a valid relevance to my present purpose, and a beginner in literature can gain more from hearing verse than from reading it."

His father shook his head. "I don't know, son. Maybe what you are doing has value. You fooled me on the sedimentation theory, and you may fool me on this. Go. Your mind is made up. You're a Haldane, and nothing I can do can change it."

He came early to the lecture hall and seated himself on a back row to study the faces of arrivals. As he had surmised, fully eighty per cent of the students in attendance were A–7s, and practically all the full professionals, though without insignia, had the A–7 look, a preoccupied dreaminess; and long-handled cigarette holders were standard equipment for the smokers.

Most of the students came in clusters to the seats, and after the house lights had dimmed, there was an inrush of students from the lobby. He had not spotted Helix, but the bulk of the students came after the lights were dimmed and he was confident that she was among the shadowy figures.

When the light at the lectern came on and the lecturer walked out from the wings, Haldane turned his entire attention to the speaker, a diminutive, bald-headed man in his late sixties with ears that jutted from his head. He leaned back from the lectern and spoke with a voice surprisingly powerful for so small a man.

"My name is Moran. I'm a professor here. My field and my subject for tonight, is the romantic poets of England. As for myself, in the dim past my people came

23

from Ireland. Our family history says that we were barred from the priesthood because a leprechaun got into the Moran cabbage patch. Do you believe that?"

The audience laughed agreement.

"So much for me. Now, for the poets. I will name them and let them speak for themselves."

Moran did precisely what he said he would.

His readings, delivered in a clear, compelling voice, went beyond meanings and grasped moods and emotions in the lines. Haldane knew from the opening sentence of the first poem that the professor had him hooked.

Moran's recitation leaped ravines no theory of aesthetics could ever bridge. Helix, in all her beauty and with all her enthusiasm, was only dawn's glow compared to this man's full sunrise.

Haldane heard the roar of the River Alph tumbling to a sunless sea, and he knew whom Coleridge had in mind when he wrote:

> Weave a circle round him thrice
> And close his eyes with holy dread,
> For he on honey-dew hath fed
> And drunk the Milk of Paradise.

Lord Byron spoke to him personally.

He had thought himself fortunate that Keats had died young. In the darkened auditorium, he mourned, now, the death of a poet who could speak with such poignancy and describe with such sweet exactitude "La Belle Dame sans Merci."

Shelley sang to him. Wordsworth comforted him. His heart danced to the skirling Scottish pipes of Burns.

When the house lights went on and the crowd rose to leave, the mood lingered. There was no hum of voices and no applause. Haldane moved quickly to the lobby to await the exit of Helix.

Eyes that caught his own returned his gaze with gentle sadness, but the eyes of Helix were not among them.

He turned and walked out of the lobby and down the mall into the crisp evening, his feet crunching softly on the fallen leaves. He paused for a moment at the fountain near the center of the campus and said softly to himself:

> And this is why I sojourn here
>   Alone and palely loitering
> Though sedge is withered from the lake,
>   And no birds sing.

He drew his cloak more tightly around him against the chill and turned the collar up, noticing his shadow sprawled over the granite flagstones surrounding the fountain.

It was a Byronesque shadow, and well it should be. He was one with Byron, with Keats, with Shelley. He had come to find his beloved and had found, instead, the living loves of dead men; yet he was alone.

Earth weary, companioned by poignancy, he turned and walked over the sere grass and beneath the stark limbs of trees that whispered in the winds of late November. He was a ghost drifting among ghosts, for he was no longer Haldane IV of the twentieth century. Helix had introduced him, and Moran had wedded him, to the immortal dead. Only his body trudged this desolate heath; his soul danced a minuet in an eighteenth-century drawing room.

He found his car and drove back to the apartment.

His father had not arrived. Remembering the disappointment he had caused the old man, Haldane went to the bureau and removed the chess pieces, setting them up for a game.

Greystone wasn't one to talk forever. His father should be in early enough for a game. Haldane, in a spirit of repentance, knew in advance that his father would win tonight.

Haldane III entered, bringing the chill on his overcoat and rubbing his hands together. His eyes lighted when he saw the chess board. "Ready for a beating?"

"Ready to give you one."

"Good. How was your lecture?"

"So-so," Haldane said. "How was yours?"

"Excellent. I've got the Fairweather Effect down pat.

How about mixing me a drink while I make room for it."

Haldane went to the bar and poured two drinks.

His father, divested of his coat, returned and pulled up a chair to the chess table. "So, your lecture was only fair. Mine was good, very good."

Well into the game, Haldane sat silent and moody until his father remarked, "I can't understand why you young people all want to jump your categories."

"Uh-huh."

"There was an art student at the lecture tonight. A girl. They introduced me as an honored guest before the lecture, and she came over and introduced herself. We sat and talked quite a while, and she listened to me. More than I can say for my son."

"Uh-huh. What'd she look like? . . . Check."

"What difference does it make? A female's a female."

"I was just wondering if my old man still had an eye for a frail."

"As you have often had the kindness to point out, son, I'm not too observant. But, as I remember, this girl had chestnut hair, hazel eyes, a rather broad face, and a determined chin. Her nose tilted slightly. Her breasts were high and wide apart. She walked with a slight sway to her hips that would have doubled her income if she had been a prostitute."

He looked over at his son with a half-grin. "Do you want me to tell you about the mole under her left breast and the appendix scar about four inches below her navel?"

Haldane looked at him seriously, "Father, I've never before truly gauged the extent of your satyriasis."

"She had beauty, a strange beauty. It seemed to be a quality of the mind as much as the body, and as I talked to her I had the impression I was talking to a much older woman. She was writing a paper on the poetry of Fairweather, and I told her about you."

"She must have made an impression if you were willing to clank out the family skeleton."

"She did. I invited her to dinner tomorrow night. She doesn't have far to come. She's a student at Golden Gate.

26

I told her I would try to get you to join us if you weren't away at some poetry lecture."

"I'll try to make it," Haldane said.

Chapter Three

SHE GLITTERED AS COLDLY AS THE NORTHERN LIGHTS, and the eyes which laughed for his father turned on him with immaculate propriety. "If your machine should work, citizen, all you would need do would be to reverse the input, and you would have an electronic poet. Such a device would destroy my category.

"Logically, the next step would be machines to create machines, and there would be no social need for human beings. Don't you agree, sir?"

"Absolutely, Helix. I told him it was a foolish idea."

Haldane had never found his father more quick to agree, had never seen him more charming or animated. The light from the old man's eyes practically illuminated the table. Outflanked, Haldane withdrew into dessert and silence as his father launched a monologue.

"You've touched on an idea that we in the department have already taken under consideration, the inadvisability of removing the human element entirely from the manipulation of machinery. Once, an invention came before the board for review . . ."

Haldane noted the phrase, "we in the department." His father was preening. Ordinarily he said merely "the department."

When they were introduced in the living room, she had said, "Citizen, your father tells me you are interested in poetry."

"Only by association."

"One would expect you to attend only mathematics lectures."

He had entered the dining room with a singing heart

and his faith in the law of averages restored. She had been seeking him at the mathematics lectures while he was seeking her.

Now, as his father talked, Haldane's thoughts vibrated between mathematics and analytics. She had about her a quality of freshness, half aetherial, half of earth, which reminded him of spring grass rising between patches of melting snow, and the vivacity of her thoughts were caught in the nuances of her face.

She was a logical impossibility. He knew that she must have liver and lungs and a thorax that functioned as those of any girl, but the whole was greater than the parts.

He leaned over and refilled his father's wine glass.

Haldane III diverted his attention from the girl long enough to ask, "Are you trying to get me drunk in order to impress our guest with your wit and brilliance while I sleep?"

"Would you care for water instead?"

Haldane had offered alternatives to ensure a choice. He cared little what his father drank as long as he drank.

As his father watched him pour, Helix said, "If you're determined to be a vivisectionist of poetry, citizen, perhaps you might be interested in its birth. As a class project, I'm writing a poem about Fairweather I, and I need help in translating his mathematics into words. Your father tells me you have an understanding of his works."

"Indeed, citizen," Haldane answered, "rather than destroy my father's confidence, I'll rush into the library after the meal and write a one paragraph explanation of his Simultaneity Theorem and draw a diagram demonstrating the Fairweather Effect. The last is simple, really. He merely uses quarks to jump the time warp."

Haldane III interrupted. "I'd like to see us mathematicians get some of the adulation given to the sociologists and psychologists, but I hardly think Fairweather would make a good subject."

"Why, Dad?"

"Among other things, he dealt with hardware, instruments and physical phenomena. He was somewhat of a manual worker, not entirely a pure theorist. . . . I wouldn't advise Fairweather as a subject. . . . Would you excuse me a moment, Helix?"

As his father rose to leave, Haldane made a rapid decision. Of late his research had led him to believe more and more in the validity of his mathematics of aesthetics, but he had put too much effort in his search for the girl to be thwarted by his integrity. Before Haldane III had passed through the door, Haldane IV had conquered his principles.

He leaned forward. "I'll help you."

"I knew you would."

"Listen, Helix. I've got to talk fast. . . . Something happened to me that day on Point Sur. Ever since, I've felt like a charged electrode without a negative pole. I've been unhappy and happy about it. Am I an atavistic poet or a Neanderthal mathematician? You're an expert. You tell me."

Her facile face revealed gentle understanding and gleeful amazement. "You've fallen in love with me!"

"I haven't fallen anywhere! I've soared like an acid-head skylark. Shelley, Keats, Byron, I know how they felt. I'm a nova to their street lamps. . . . I've got the black belt!"

"Oh, no," she shook her head. "The primitives knew all about what you have, and they called it 'puppy love.' But it's merely a symptom. If the germ incubates properly it develops into what the primitives called 'mature companionship,' where the male and female enjoy being together."

"Oh, no," Haldane demurred, thinking there were gaps in her knowledge, "I know about that, but this is in my mind. I enjoy just looking at you, and touching you."

He reached over and took her hand. "It's fun just to hold your hand."

"Unhand me," she whispered, "before your father returns."

He complied, noticing that she could have drawn her own hand back just as easily, but she had not. He slumped back in his chair. "I wanted to tell you something about my heart being like a singing bird, but it didn't come out that way."

He did not know the human voice could carry such gentleness until he heard her answer. "Don't worry, Haldane. You've told me more than you know, and every morning of my life will start with the song of your acidhead skylark."

Three valuable seconds ticked by in silence. Helix was the first to speak. "Forget you're a stuttering poet and be the precise mathematician. Figure, quickly, some way to help me write the epic of Fairweather, for I'll never help you ungild the lilies of my heart."

He had long since planned his answer.

"Meet me in the morning, at nine o'clock, at the fountain on your campus."

She nodded, and lifted her coffee to her lips as his father re-entered the room.

Haldane arose at seven Sunday morning and took almost an hour to shave twice, trim his nails and toenails, shower, soap, rinse, resoap, rerinse, dry himself, splash his face with aftershave lotion and dry his hands on his bare chest. He was sparing of the hair cream, using just enough to give his hair a sheen.

Naked before his mirror, he stood for a moment flexing muscles made lithe by judo training. He selected the grey tunic flecked with silver thread with the silver *M–5* stitched above the left breast, his matching overcoat with the pale silver lining, and his grey boots of reinforced chamois. His trousers were of grey, fleece-lined denim with a triple-stitched codpiece.

Dressed and standing before the mirror, he reluctantly admitted that he looked every inch the eighteenth-century boudoir hero. His thin, sensitive face reminded him of John Keats, except for the hair. That full, blond thatch, with a mere innuendo of a wave, was Byronesque, and the eyes, cool, gray, and objective, focused with the calculating ease of a pragmatist to the empirical method born.

Donning his overcoat with a flourish, he wheeled and strode into the kitchen, where he doffed the coat and breakfasted standing up and bent far over the bar lest crumbs stain the burnished sheen of his tunic.

Redonning the overcoat, he departed the ancestral demesne, knowing the patriarch, slumbering in his chambers, would awaken to assume his son had gone for early mass, and Dad would be three-fourths correct.

Enroute to the campus, he drove beside the marina. On his left, the pastel towers mounted Nob and Russian Hills. On his right, a fresh breeze spanked the buttocks of wavelets undulating atop the bay. Above him, clouds no bigger than the breasts of girls accentuated the blue. It was a brisk, stimulating eighteenth-century day.

He parked and cut across the campus through the trees. As he neared the fountain, the film of branches thinned with decreasing distance, and he saw her.

She was standing by the fountain reading a book, wearing a shawl instead of a cape and dressed in a skirt that had obviously been ironed under her mattress.

Chagrined by his own finery, he edged from the cover of the trees.

She looked up and smiled, extending her hand as he neared her. He bowed and kissed the hand.

"Spare me the chivalry, Haldane," she said, withdrawing her hand quickly. "We have bird-watchers on this campus."

"I wore my Sunday go-to-mass clothes."

"I felt you would," she said, "so I dressed differently to keep people from assuming we had been to church together."

"You're as clever as you are fair. Are you chilly?"

"A little."

"What are the books?"

"The thin one's the poetic works of Fairweather, and the heavy one's an anthology of nineteenth-century poetry."

"Oh," he said, trying to hide his resentment of the books. He had almost forgotten the reason for their meeting, and the reminder was disappointing. It was as if she had brought little brother along.

"We don't have to talk about them in this cold," he said, and explained to her about Malcolm's apartment and how he had come to acquire it. He gave a verbatim report of his conversation with his roommate without editorializing on the motives behind his conversation.

She thought the idea sensible.

"You take the big book and walk north, and I'll go back the way I came. If we're being watched, whoever sees us will think we met for me to give you a textbook. Now handle the book with care, for it's a family heirloom. I'll delay for a few minutes before I go to the apartment."

"Dad didn't care for your choice of subject, did you notice?"

"I expected his reaction."

"How so?"

"I'll tell you at the apartment."

"You're not frightened?"

"I am, a little," she confessed.

"The risks are only as great as we make them."

"It's not our meeting being reported that I fear. It's something else, more important, that I've found in the books. Go now, but don't look back."

He turned and strolled down the mall, whistling. To any casual onlooker he was merely a student who had borrowed a book from another student and gone about his business.

He whistled to allay his own concern. On her face he had seen a deep-seated anxiety rather than a passing fear. Whatever it might be that she had found in the books, she was troubled.

Helix was impressed by the Malcolm apartment.

After she had taken off her coat and laid the books on the divan, she bubbled with comments. "Look at the gorgeous view! . . . Isn't this carving adorable? . . . I thought you were supposed to dust!"

He had not seen the apartment since his first inspection. He shrugged his shoulders. "It needs a woman's touch, and so do I."

She was gazing out the window as he walked up behind her and put his arms about her. She turned to him, her face tilted.

He kissed her.

Heretofore, he had never particularly valued a kiss as a thing in itself. Mates and brothers and sisters kissed. The kiss had not been one of the major weapons in his arsenal; in fact, he had deplored the ritual as unsanitary although he had bowed to the convention. Kissing this girl was definitely pleasant, and he was lingering to the point of procrastination when she pushed him back.

To his chagrin and consternation, he saw that her face was set in the impersonal lines of formality, and her voice was flat as she recited: "As a female citizen bearing on my tunic the insignia of the professional, it is my duty to hold the seed within me sacred to the purposes of the state. I shall be feminine at all times but at no time womanly except in the presence of the mate selected for me by the Department of Genetics."

She paused, now, looking at him, rather than through him, and her eyes flicked downward for a split second. "We are not going to risk declassification. One of us has to be strong, and some instinct tells me it will not be you."

Standing before her, he knew his plans had gone awry, not so much by what she had said as by the way he felt. His reaction to her had been total.

She was to the girls at Belle's Place what a philharmonic orchestra was to a banjo, but an orchestra had a string section and in his response to the nuances and range of the emotions she aroused in him, he took pride rather than shame in the tremor which had frightened her. He desired her with self-admitted desire encompassed by a greater desire to guard her from harm. He would never permit the blithe lad he had been two months before to carry out his plan and endanger this girl.

So he donned his mask and answered her, "I agree with you, citizen, that it is folly for a professional to endanger the social welfare for a tremor in the loins . . ."—he paused at the familiar phrase, and heard his voice, as something apart from him, veer off from his recital of the creed— ". . . even though that tremor might be the expression of the highest sentiments of the human heart and be as free from the dross of flesh as an eagle in its flight."

He resumed the creed: ". . . and he who is willing to sacrifice so much for so little has tarnished his honor and his dynastic line, and traduced the state."

33

Suddenly he grinned, and a wild authority rang in his voice. "I agree with you because you're such an agreeable girl, but if you were to lean forward and whisper, 'Come, Haldane, defrock and deflower me,' I would agree with you, also, and with a helluva lot fewer words."

She laughed outright.

"You've heard both versions," he said, "mine and theirs. Remember my version, won't you? You can get the official version from those silverfish at Golden Gate when their hands start fluttering accidentally against your hips."

"Why, silly, you're jealous!"

"I'm not jealous! It makes me crave soda-water when I think that some of those alleged males probably come early to classes to watch you walk in and stay late to walk out behind you. And the profs aren't above a little hoggle-oggling, either. I bet you could get straight A's if you wrote your answers in Sanskrit."

She was giggling as she pointed an imperious finger at the sofa. "Sit down! It's not the lechery of poets that I fear; it's the virility of mathematicians."

She sat down, at the far end of the sofa, and said, "We've got to establish policy. No more Sunday meetings. I spend my Sundays in Sausalito with my parents, and a break in habit patterns would be suspicious. No telephone calls. Phone calls only, and let those be short. And we should limit our meetings to one hour only on Saturday. And we should stagger the time of the meetings, setting the time each preceding Saturday."

"You're shrewd," he said.

"I'll have to be. If anyone in authority found out about this and assumed the worst, we could be psychoanalyzed."

"I don't want to go through that, again," he said.

"You have been, then?"

"Mother fell out of the window when she was watering flower pots on the ledge. I was a child when it happened. I didn't know better, so I blamed the flower pots. When I pushed them off the ledge with a broomstick, one of them hit a pedestrian. I was analyzed for aggressions."

"You must have had a student analyst," she said. "But

back to now. Have you read any of Fairweather's poetry?"

"No, and deliberately no. I'm not out of the woods in the eighteenth century, yet. Your boy, Moran, helped me a lot, but when I come to the master, I want to understand his language."

"You've certainly overestimated the poetic power of our noble hero." She handed him the small volume. "Open it and read to me at random any quatrain."

He opened the book and read:

> It was so cold the snow squeaked underfoot
>   And random gusts drew skirrs
> From surface snow which skittered off the scree
>   To eddy into drifts against the firs.

"His language isn't difficult," she said, "is it?"

"He uses a few words that I wouldn't use in talking, but the reason I wouldn't use them is that my friends wouldn't understand me if I did."

"What do you think of the subject?"

"The snow scene? . . . I like it. I've always had a weakness for snow so hard it skirred when it skittered off a scree. None of this mushy slush for me, that goes 'slurp' when it hits."

"But there are no symbols," she protested.

"Some folks like symbols. Some don't. I can't stand symbols in snow scenes. I like my snow pure and unadulterated."

"A poem should mean something besides the obvious," she said. "Now, turn to page 83."

He turned to the page to find the familiar title, "Reflections from a Higher Place, Revised." But there were only four of the lines she had quoted at Point Sur, their depth augmented by decorative rows of asterisks.

```
***************************
```
> He tells us, standing on His place,
> That he who loses wins the race,
> That hemlock has a pleasant taste,
> That parallel lines must meet in space
```
***************************
```

35

"You told me you thought it was the Sermon on the Mount," she said, when he looked up from the page, "and the editor thought so, too. The editor capitalized 'He' and took out the lines about blessing by murder which wouldn't have been appropriate for Jesus.

"Another item: asterisks usually mean deletions. The editor makes them resemble decorations which suggests to me that he was arranging a cover story for his act. If someone were to come to him and say, 'Look, this isn't a complete poem,' then he could say, 'Yes, but I made a note of it. See the asterisks.'

"The man who would have had to say that, the editor of that volume, is the chief of the Department of Literature. His signature makes the work authoritative. But why would the head of the department edit a book by an obscure poet?"

"Fairweather was a state hero," Haldane reminded her.

"But not in poetry. Furthermore, the title of that book is *The Complete Poetic Works of Fairweather I*. That title is completely false."

"Girl, you're accusing a state authority of censorship and misrepresentation."

"Precisely. It's horrifying, but it's true! Take the other book, carefully, and you'll find another Fairweather poem in it, a poem not even mentioned in *The Complete Poetic Works*.

"That book is an anthology of nineteenth-century poetry. It's been out of print for over a hundred years, a family heirloom, and it's probably the only copy in the world. Look on page 286."

He turned to the page carefully. The sheets were brittle with age, but the old letterpress type was still beautifully legible.

He found the poem. Its title alone would have stamped it as pure Fairweather: "Lament of a Grounded Star Rover."

> You could trace our course through the Milky Way
> By our wake of thundering light,
> But they called us home as we heeled the keel
> Round Ursa Minor's bight.

36

(The Weird Sisters had taken, they said,
  The web of the galaxy
To weave it into fairer strands
  On the loom of destiny.)

Uranus had been to our dragon ship
  As the Pillar of Hercules,
And Orion's flare was a beacon buoy
  That led to the Pleiades,

Where veiled Merope mourns apart
  And scans the skies in vain
For her mortal loves who returned to her,
  But come not back again.

You err but once when you ride the light.
  Stout hearts must con that helm.
All men grow sad and some go mad,
  For the voids can overwhelm.

But, God, if I could, I would launch my keel
  And dare, again, that sea;
For the Weird Sisters have taken my stars
  To weave a shroud for me.

As Haldane bent his head to the page, his mind grasped the first image of the poem—it was accurate and true with more than truth to think of a laser ship throwing behind it a wake of thundering light—and suddenly he too was yearning for the far sweep of the stars, bemoaning the final betrayal of Merope, she who loved a mortal and so died, and regretting and resenting the shroud that had been woven for the valiant old star rover who wanted to go back, even if it meant space madness and death. Giants had walked this earth a century ago.

But Helix wanted symbols. . . . Merope, of course, represented the lost dreams of romance, a fact he would not have recognized two months earlier.

"Did you find any symbolism?"

Urgency in her question turned it into a plea. She was looking to him for reassurance that the state was all-benign and truthful as she had been taught.

"Merope was one of the Seven Sisters who fell in love with a mortal and was exiled from heaven. . . ."

"And the three Weird Sisters are the fates," she said,

almost impatiently, "but those are mythical allusions, a method of writing that went out of style with that impossible John Milton.

"I'm concerned because this anthology is on microfilm, and data analysis would have produced the poem from the archives when Fairweather's poetic works were being compiled. Can you see any reason why this poem should be censored?"

He had not known that there were three Weird Sisters. Helix was confusing herself by poetic forms. There was nothing in the book to prevent Fairweather from turning an allusion into a symbol. With growing awareness of the meaning of the poem, he realized what Fairweather had done.

"You overlook one fact, Helix," he said. "Editors edit. No editor would include this jingle in a work of poetry."

His idea registered, and she relaxed.

"I think you're right, Haldane. Yes, I'm sure you are. And the deletions could have been made for the same reason. For a while, I had begun to suspect censorship, which would mean there was something rotten in the state of the State."

She was visibly relaxed now, her intelligence and her conditioning reintegrated.

"Next Saturday, I suggest we meet at ten. I'd like you to help me consider the rhyme scheme I should use in my poem. To brush up on the background, I'll check out the official biography of Fairweather, and I'd like to suggest that you read in the general history of Fairweather's times.

"Meanwhile, I'm afraid we're going to have to use this period for the cleaning of the apartment. In the six weeks you've been coming here, you must have intended the dust to lie fallow for next year's crop."

As he rummaged in the broom closet for the dust mops, Haldane's face was set in lines of serious thought.

He knew who the Weird Sisters were, and he knew what Merope meant, and he knew with unequivocal certainty that the poem had been censored. The symbols

Helix missed were there in all their dreadful implication: there was something rotten in the state of the State.

After they parted, Haldane did not go home immediately. He drove to the entrance of the Golden Gate Bridge and walked onto the span, choosing the ocean side.

For more than an hour he leaned against the guard rail and watched a fog bank roll in from the ocean. It moved slowly, a sheer-faced cliff of mist from beneath which the ocean pulsated, coming toward him in widely separated rollers that slapped the pontoons beneath him with a *sough-sough.*

On his left the Presidio was finally lost in the shroud, and at his right the western slope of Tamalpais went under, but it was the ocean which fascinated him most; flat, oily, sinister, it pulsated from beneath the fog bank.

Once that sea had called to men and men had answered, but that was long ago, long, long ago. Then, monsters had slithered in its depth and winds had tortured its surface, but the men had come, and the breed of man who challenged the sea had died with the sea's terrors. Now, the only men who plied its routes were the sailors of the freighter submarines which glided fathoms below, indifferent to the storms that moiled the surface.

Then space had called, and there were men who would have answered, but the Weird Sisters had canceled the probes and the stars which should have been the new universe of man had become man's shroud.

He stood on the apex of man's destiny, in the best of all possible societies on the best of all possible planets, yet some atomy in his being still cried for worlds to conquer. He was not satisfied. Ineffable longings stirred a fever in his blood.

He longed for Helix with yearnings beyond Helix, for she had triggered forces in the chambers of his mind where the darkness was seeking light.

As the wisps of fog curled over the bridge, growing thicker, flicking on the bridge lights, he turned and walked back toward the land. His footsteps sounded hollow on the deserted bridge, and he felt intensely alone.

For a moment, he felt he was not returning to San Francisco but entering a dark land peopled by hostile men. Without inner prompting, a line of overwhelming immediacy leaped from the thousands of lines he had read in the past months, a fragment accentuating his exile from a suddenly alien earth, and he spoke the line aloud into the fog:

"Childe Roland to the dark tower came. . . ."

Chapter Four

HELIX PHONED HIM ON FRIDAY.

He was alone in the room after taking a shower when his phone buzzed. Assuming some schoolmate was calling, he took it from the pocket of his robe and said, "Haldane."

He was startled to hear her voice, saying, "Citizen, I'm sorry to inform you that the volume you requested is on the proscribed list."

His voice held no pretense at cool officiousness as he blurted out, "Madam, he built the pope!"

"Nevertheless, his biography is proscribed. Citizen, you realize this will interfere with the project."

He cared not an icicle on Hell for the project, but with nothing to justify their meetings, Helix might cancel them.

Suddenly his voice rang with authority, "I have other sources of information, Madam. Will you be open Saturday?"

"If arrangements are made beforehand, we open on Saturday. I believe you have an appointment, have you not?"

"Yes."

"Then I have a suggestion for a secondary topic which I hope to offer to you tomorrow."

"Thank you, Madam, and good day."

He sat on the edge of his bed, seething and angry with the sense of a man who has been defrauded by a petty trickster.

He could understand why no one had mentioned that Fairweather wrote poetry. It was information not germane to his subjects, and he had never asked the question. But this was different.

He had spent two years here, studying the ideas of a man who had contributed more to mathematics than Euclid or Einstein, a man who had contributed more to theology than Saint Augustine, a man buried in a hero's grave in Arlington, yet he had never read a subordinate clause in a footnote in any text which hinted that Fairweather had ever been under a cloud from the Church.

Was history a state secret?

He had an ace, and he would play it.

Haldane III, as a department member, would have access to such information. Two weeks ago he would have asked his father straight from the shoulder why the Church had the gall to proscribe the biography of the man who had assembled the last representative of Saint Peter on earth, but now he would have to move with circumspection. Haldane III might suspect from the question that his son had continued an illicit relation with their dinner guest.

Such suspicions might prove fatal to his plans. If his premonition on the bridge last Sunday was true, his father would be in the enemy's camp.

On his way home, he stopped by a sporting-goods store to make a purchase and arrived after his father. During dinner, Haldane challenged him to chess. "To make it worth my time, I'll play you double stakes."

He almost made a tactical error. His father jumped at the offer, and Haldane won the first game. The double gin was so potent that it almost rendered him incapable of losing the second.

His father won the third game so decisively that he was able to remark, "Chess separates the mathematicians from the ribbon clerks."

After two more victories, Haldane III was criticizing his son's whole system of play with sweeping grandeur. "Attack! Aggressiveness is the spirit of the game, and the queen is the crux. Chess is a matriarchy built on the power of the female, and whoever cannot control the power of the female loses his virility, is emasculated as a chess player."

Haldane appreciated his father's comments because he was needing all the assistance he could get in figuring out losing moves.

Meanwhile, he was gathering courage to steer the conversation into areas that would help him solve the riddle of Fairweather's proscription.

To maintain a semblance of a contest, he won, and tapped his courage from the same barrel from which sloshed his father's omniscience on chess. He suddenly realized he was wasting vast amounts of tact and diplomacy on a conversation which Haldane III would not even remember on the morrow.

"Dad, why is the official biography of Fairweather proscribed?"

"Maybe because he experimented with antimatter?"

"He lived before the experiments were outlawed."

"You're right! Your move."

Haldane moved his king, putting it in jeopardy.

His father studied the board.

"Then why was it proscribed?"

"He got into a fight with Pope Leo XXXV. Leo tried to excommunicate him. But the sociologists backed Fairweather. Not that they liked Fairweather, mind you. They figured Leo was bucking for more power. He was a popular pope. With the faithful behind him, who knows?"

Haldane waited excruciating moments while his father did not check the king when he finally moved.

"But a pope wouldn't bring excommunication proceedings against a state hero without a powerful reason."

"You're absodamnlutely right, son. Your move."

Haldane moved his king into checkmate on the line with his father's queen, but his father moved a pawn diagonally and blocked the check.

Haldane moved one back and two over with his castle.

42

"Why did they let him invent the pope?"

"Big struggle going on in the triumvirate back in those days. Soc and Psych ganged up on the Church. They welcomed Fairweather's invention. Henry VIII, the head sociologist, knew he sure as hell didn't have to worry about political maneuvering on the part of a computer. . . . Check!"

Haldane castled for the third time.

"Why did Leo want to censure Fairweather?"

"State secret, son. Your move."

"I just moved, Dad. I castled."

"If it's all so confidential, why is his biography simply proscribed?"

"It was degutted first. Proscription was just a sop to the Church."

It had taken a high degree of skill mixed with illegal moves to do it, but he had his father in a position where any move he made would result in checkmating his son. There was a mocking half-smile on Haldane III's face, a silent cry of impending triumph, as he studied the board. Haldane cut through the train of delicious thoughts that were coupling in the old man's mind and asked, "Do you think you could get that biography for me? It might be interesting."

"Get it yourself," he waved an impatient hand toward his study. "It's in there, on the top shelf. . . . Check-mate!"

He came early to the Malcolm apartment to check for hidden microphones and to arrange a dozen roses he had brought in a brass urn near the foyer. When he finished his tasks, he sat down on the sofa and began to reread the biography he had read into the late hours of the night before.

He heard her pause by the roses when she entered, and he pretended to be engrossed in the book. He looked up to see her rearranging the flowers. "They should be spread more. This old patriarch should be given the dominant position."

With a few movements, she was transforming his lump-ish arrangement into a harmonized design.

43

He walked over and kissed her neck. "Personification is a poor literary device."

"The teacher is being taught. You're clever."

"Clever, quick, and devious." He steered her to the sofa and pointed to the book he had laid there. She reached down and picked it up, almost with awe. "His biography."

"Dad lent it to me."

"Surely you didn't talk to him about Fairweather?"

"He won't remember. The doctor recommended a drink or two before bedtime for his hypertension. Last night was very tranquil."

Vexation fretted his face. "If he were a man of loose faculties, he never would have been named to the department."

"He had sense enough not to talk about state secrets. He almost did, and then he clammed up."

"Did he tell you why the biography was proscribed?"

"As a sop to the Church. Pope Leo tried to excommunicate him, but Soc and Psych stopped the pope."

"Does the biography discuss the incident?"

He looked away.

Last Sunday she had been horrified by the thought that the state was capable of practicing censorship in the best of all possible worlds, and he had lied to protect her beliefs. Her life had been conditioned to the belief that the state was all-benevolent, and he wondered if he had the right to test that belief, to endanger her sanity.

But she was a professional, not Pavlov's dog, and she was dedicated to the search for truth. Did he have the right to censor unpleasant truths in his dealings with her? If he remained silent, he would become an ally of that which he contested and dishonor the mystique which bound him to her.

Deliberately, he answered. "It mentions the incident only in general terms. You see, Helix, before the Fairweather biography was proscribed, it was censored."

"You know there is censorship, then?"

"I've known it since last Sunday," he admitted.

He thought he saw relief flicker in her eyes, but the emotion was lost in an expression of concern—for him.

44

"Then you know who the three Weird Sisters are?" Her voice was flat and unemotional.

"Yes," he answered.

"I was worried for you," she said, relaxing. "They condition you so strongly."

She had been protecting him.

Suddenly her manner changed, and she was brisk, business-like. "So the biography gives no hint of Pope Leo's reasons for attempting Fairweather's excommunication?"

"It doesn't even call it excommunication. It says he was threatened with possible censure. Semantically, the statement's true. Excommunication is a form of censure, a very final form.

"However, it does say, 'for reasons of alleged moral turpitude.' "

"Another one of those phrases," she said, impatiently, "but tell me, how long after this censure did he complete the pope?"

"He was censured in 1850, and the pope was placed in the new Holy See in 1881."

"Thirty years he labored in the vineyards of Our Lord even though the pope had tried to eject him."

"This will interest you. He was married to a proletarian."

"When?" she asked.

"1822. They had a son. The biography doesn't mention him except to say he was entered as a professional in the department of mathematics. Obviously, the dynasty ended with the son."

"That doesn't interest me as much as the thirty years he spent in the service of the Church, although that proletarian marriage suggests an individualism which might have led to deviationism."

"Not a chance," Haldane said. "Soc and Psych would have never sided with a deviationist against the Church."

"But why should he give his loyalties to the very department which attempted to destroy him?"

"Maybe the pope was out to get him, so he got the pope, the living one, I mean."

"Hate isn't strong enough to drive a man for thirty years to do what he did. Only love could do that, or remorse.

"Haldane, let me read the book. Perhaps, reasoning together, we might be able to find the answer."

"If we find the wrong answer," he said, "the project might be blocked. . . . You mentioned a subsidiary project on the phone. What was your idea?"

"My idea doesn't have to be considered now that you've got a copy of the biography, but I thought I might prepare a paper on the techniques and emotional reactions of an eighteenth-century lover. Since you're in love with me, you would have made an ideal subject-partner."

"You mean, I was to act out the role?"

"That was the general idea. . . . I wanted to test some of the techniques that the coquettes used—'flirting,' they called it—to heighten the excitement of their lovers."

If he had known that was her plan, he swore inwardly, he would never have brought the book!

Calmly he said, "That plan is still valid. In writing the poem, I could have helped you little except in the research. And the subject can still thwart us. We can't reveal state secrets we aren't supposed to know about, even in a symbol, without alerting the triumvirate, but I could have given you a great deal of first-hand information about the techniques and reactions of eighteenth-century lovers. As a matter of fact, I'm a gold mine of original material on that subject."

"Demonstrate."

"To begin with, there was the romantic kiss, like this."

He embraced her and shoved her back on the divan, not kissing her lips, but moving from her clavicle toward her chin, mincing his lips rapidly in the manner of a saxophonist triple-tongueing his instrument. She grabbed his hair in her hand, twisted his head around, and nibbled on her ear.

He felt chagrin because she had stolen his next move from him. He stood up, relaxed, nonchalant, walked over to his tunic, and pulled out a cigarette. "Do you smoke?" he asked.

"No, but if you do, the filter goes in your mouth."

She was giggling, and as he flipped the cigarette, he knew, inexpert as he was at this type of experiment, that she would never be in the right mood if she was laughing. To call her attention to the barometer reading, he said, "The old romantics practiced a form of self-control which was called 'yoga.' In a way it was a religion. I picked up a little of it in my studies on the subject."

He doused the cigarette after one slow puff, snubbed it in the tray, and sat down beside her, one arm casually draped over the back of the divan behind her. "Interesting religion, yoga."

"Did they put their arm around a girl and talk about religion?"

"Of course. They called it 'small talk.' Sometimes it was politics, sometimes it was world affairs. Most often it was religion."

"Your research doesn't jibe with mine."

"Straighten your legs out so I can see the dimples on your knees."

"I didn't read about that, either."

"Your knee caps are very pretty. Kick your sandals off so I can see your toes. . . . That's right. Five and five, ten pretty little pinkies. . . . This is flattery I'm giving you now."

He reached down and put his hand over the kneecap closest to him. "I'm just checking to see if it's all yours. . . . That's a remark they used to make to get to touch what they called secondary erogenous zones. . . ."

"Now, that's what I call small talk," she said.

His fingers tapped her kneecaps.

"You're built along the lines of a Gothic arch," he said, "with the perspective of your limbs drawing the attention upward. . . ."

"Limbs?" She interrupted.

"Archaic for legs. . . . Back to the Gothic arch: its lines were designed to draw one's attention toward heaven."

"Now is this flattery," she asked, "or is it a lecture on Gothic architecture?"

"Helix!" He patted her knee reprovingly. "You're sup-

47

posed to be a poet. That's symbolism. I'm telling you, old-style, that your sacrolumbar area is heavenly."

She shook her head. "Either you're a poor poet or I'm poor at understanding symbols. Give me another example."

"Very well. We'll consider your limbs as monads. This right one is strong, well muscled. You must do a lot of running."

"Is that supposed to be flattery?"

"In a manner," he explained. "Actually, it's what they called a veiled compliment. When a girl does a lot of running, that means she's usually being chased."

Her rigid arm around his shoulder relaxed slightly and she smiled. "Some primitive instinct tells me you're getting closer to the general area of courtship."

Encouraged, he stroked the underside of her knee and felt Gothic compulsions grasp his fingertips. "Your skin is as satiny as silk."

"Is silk satiny, or silky?" she asked, alert as always to mixed figures of speech. But he noticed a quickened tempo to her breathing which inspired him to improvisations.

"Keep your satin-fingered silkiness below the skirtline," she said and added, "Don't. Stop."

Her word-order confused him. He wondered if she meant "Don't" and "Stop" or "Don't stop." If she wanted him to stop, he reasoned, she could always push him away; instead, she was clinging more firmly than ever; almost hysterically.

"Oh, Haldane, please stop."

She was weeping, and he hadn't wished to make her cry. Besides, she was definitely asking him to stop, so he disengaged himself and arose to light another cigarette, carefully lighting the nonfiltered end. He noticed that his hand trembled slightly, and he laid the cigarette down to remove his handkerchief from his tunic. Strangely, a simple exercise in ancient courtship had given him an insight into history—he could understand the population explosion. Bending to dab her eyes, he knew that, had she been even slightly receptive, he might have committed miscegenation, despite his self-promises.

She opened her eyes and looked up at him with hostility. "Were you at one of those houses before you came here?"

Perplexed by her irrelevancy, he answered bluntly. "I haven't since Point Sur."

She must have believed him. "We were saved by yoga," she said. "I challenged your yoga, and I would have lost."

It was Haldane's turn to feel hysteria. Sitting beside her, he said, "But, Helix, there wasn't any yoga. I'm wearing an athletic supporter. I'm under restraint."

He was sliding an arm around her waist when she doubled up her fist and began to pound him on the chest, weeping again. "You beast! You crude, deceitful beast. All the time, you let me think it was I. All the time, I was trying to beat yoga. . . ."

She quit pounding him and dropped her face to her hands, sobbing. Gently he reached over, placed an arm over her shoulders, and reassured her, "Helix, you whipped him to a frazzle."

She threw his arm away and jumped to her feet, walked over to a chair, sat down, and glared at him. "Don't you ever touch me again, you beast."

His mind whirled. She was genuinely angry with him because he had obeyed her a moment before, and once he had explained why, she had become angry with him for doing what she had formerly been angry with him for not doing. He threw up his hands in despair. "Helix, let's look at this matter rationally," he said, "and forget the eighteenth century. Come back and let me hold your hand, and I'll apologize for my deceit and my irrational behavior. There are a few other refinements of the ritual which might enlighten you when it comes to writing. . . ."

She shook her head stubbornly. "No, if it happened once, it would happen again. You're in love, you nut. Here"—she reached down, picked up the Fairweather biography, and tossed it toward him—"read about your god, you saint of mathematics."

"I have no gods. I'm a born loser, and the gods were all triumphant. Jesus, Fairweather, Jehovah, they're all winners. The only ball team I cheer is the Baltimore Orioles.

Only one moment of my life was granted me to look on the face of beauty, and beauty thumbed her nose."

She was not listening. Her eyes were looking away and fuming. Her kneecaps, primly touching, pointed away from him.

He sat mute, Fairweather forgotten on his aching lap.

Finally, she rose and went into the foyer, looking down on him with haughty coolness, holding herself primly erect and more than an arm's length from him as she passed, her hips not swaying half an inch from the perpendicular. As she passed into the foyer, her hands swooped over the vase of roses, touching them lightly with a caress of infinite grace.

She came back into the room carrying a guitar, moving with wariness past the couch where he sat. She resumed her seat in the chair, and the lines of her body relaxed in soft arcs around the instrument. As she hummed a note and struck the strings, she reminded him of a painting, madonna and child, until she looked over at him and her lips curled silently around the word, "Beast!"

He watched her tune the instrument, her deft fingers flicking over the bridge, her ears cocked for the sounds. Every movement seemed impressed with her own peculiar grace, and it was delightful to sit and watch her even though she was pouting and angry.

Finally, she turned to him. "I wanted to sing you some old English and Scottish ballads to demonstrate a very simple meter in the same context as the ancient epic poems, that is, oral. Originally, poetry was written to be chanted. I planned to do this to give you some flavor of the preromantic verse, but now I'm doing it to collect your wits."

At the moment, nothing could have appealed to him less than a ballad, but he did not wish to arouse the anger of this half-vixen, half-goddess, so he pretended an interest.

His interest wasn't pretended for long.

Her voice was weak and its range limited, but its enunciation was clear and its timbre low-pitched and vibrant. As all else about her, it was a wedding of opposites, husky yet plaintive.

50

She played the guitar well, and her voice was adequate for the songs she sang. Obviously, the ballads were not written for virtuosi of the voice.

Though sentimental and sad, the songs were unabashedly sentimental, and there was little morbidity in their sadness. They delighted in death and partings. "Barbry Allen" told of two who died for love, and rose trees, growing from each grave, climbed a church wall to tie themselves into a lovers' knot, a highly improbable phenomenon but charming to think about. Another spoke of a gentleman by the name of Tom Dooley who murdered a female and had to hang. With rare good humor, the crowd at the foot of his gallows exhorted him to hang down his head and cry.

Listening to her and watching her, it seemed impossible that this girl was the same who had pounded him in rage and frustration only minutes before. Mated to her, a man would know contrasts; after being emotionally tossed about by the gales of her beauty and wit, he could always enter the quiet harbors of her gentleness and her arts.

At that moment, he caught the first glimmerings of an idea which he knew was shot through with peril to himself, to her, and to their dynasties. But the idea was before him, and he had to consider it. The idea considered was a resolution made.

He would stake a legal claim on the territory of her heart. Some way, somehow, though it meant circumventing the sociologists, deluding the geneticists, and subverting the State, he was going to be legally mated to Helix.

Slowly, he lifted the official biography of Fairweather from his lap and kissed the book.

Chapter Five

CHRISTMAS CAME EARLY THAT YEAR, OR SO IT SEEMED TO the student with the vast problem. He was surprised to find that secret batches of eggnog had been prepared in the dormitories. Absently, he hummed a carol now and then, merely to keep up pretenses, as his mind probed at his problem with the fearfulness of an octopus approaching the sinking bulk of a killer whale.

To jump genetic barriers was an impossible feat. To jump them and land in a predetermined spot, out of five hundred million spots on the North American continent alone, was an impossibility cubed. Even the attempt to subvert state policies to personal ends could result in an S.O.S. at least, and in exile to the planet Hell at most.

Insanity was a relative state, and he, at least, knew he was insane. Other factors were in his favor—his father's knowledge and his growing awareness that the omniscient state was not an abstraction but an agglomeration of sociologists, psychologists, and priests, professions which ranked far lower on the Kraft-Stanford Scale of Comparative Intelligence than theoretical mathematicians.

His Great Idea struck him during a bull session in the dormitory room on the last Friday before the holidays.

Students had drifted in and out for most of the afternoon, mixing eggnog with ribaldry and jests with earnest discussions. Haldane, alone in the group, leafed through a *Lives of the Popes* he had given Malcolm as a present in exchange for a bathrobe. He had discovered that Pope Leo, the last human pope, had established the order of proletarian priests, called the Gray Brothers, who were admitted to the brotherhood without formal education in theology. It was a humanitarian act that did not mesh with his attempts to excommunicate Fairweather; Haldane, interested, called over, "Say, Mal, how about my borrowing this book over the holidays?"

"Sure, but bring it back. It's a Christmas gift."

Almost simultaneously, the guests and brandy disappeared, and Malcolm and Haldane had the room to themselves. Malcolm invited Haldane to accompany him on a skiing holiday in the Sierras. "Great fun, boy. Icy air on your cheeks, crunch of snow under your skis, and the crack of breaking legs.

"We'll hole up in Bishop. If things get dull, we can take a helitrip up to the Holy See. As long as you're practicing celibacy, you might as well get in with the priesthood. Maybe you could check the pope's circuits."

Haldane wondered if the invitation were purely social or if his roommate, sensing Haldane's nonconformist tendencies, was genuinely concerned with his spiritual welfare.

"Thanks for the invitation, but I have a lot of reading."

"Don't tell me . . . the aesthetics of mathematics . . . or is it the mathematics of aesthetics? I keep getting the input confused with the output."

As Haldane shaved preparatory to leaving for home, he remembered that Helix had pointed out the logic of reversing the input, and he knew he had already been working on the project which would put him into an entirely new category, one into which Helix could fit as easily as a cog on a meshed wheel.

He would design and build an electronic Shakespeare, one which, logically, would demand the co-development of literary cybernetics.

Helix would take cybernetics as an elective.

He sang a little tune as he finished shaving, and Malcolm, hearing him from the room, asked, "What kind of song is that?"

"One our ancestors sang."

"Bloodthirsty progenitors, we have."

He had been singing the nonsensical ditty:

> Lizzie Borden took an ax
> And gave her mother forty whacks.
> When she saw what she had done,
> She gave her father forty-one.

His singing reflected a subconscious shot through with trepidation, for he was dreading what he had to tell Helix on Saturday.

How did one graciously present a girl with an ax to kill the ancestors of her spirit?

That evening over chess, Haldane stalked his father's knowledge, using candor as a blind. "In reading Fairweather's biography, I wondered how he could mate with a worker."

"Rank has its privileges."

"When you mated, how many females did you interview?"

"Six. That's about par for a mathematician in one area. I always liked Orientals, and if I'd had rocket fare to Peking, you'd be Eurasian."

"What made you choose mother?"

"She said she could play chess. . . . Don't divert me. I think I've got you beaten."

Saturday howled into San Francisco. Russian Hill, Nob Hill, and Telegraph Hill jutted into an underbelly of clouds and were as lost as plowshares scudding through black loam. Rain squalls pounded the bay, and Alcatraz was bloated by mists.

Helix floated in like a hymn to intellectual beauty, books under her arms and ideas brimming in her eyes.

"Fairweather's trial was held in November of 1850. His mate died in February of that year. According to the mating schedule, she would have been in her mid-forties, so she did not die of natural causes. It's possible, even probable, that whatever caused her death also caused the trial. Fairweather did something terrible that year, if she jumped. Do you agree that it's a logical possibility that she jumped?"

"A logical probability. She was mated to a man whose ideas she could not have shared, because there are not fifteen men in the world today who can grasp the full implications of his theories."

"Good! Now there remains the figure of Fairweather II, their son. He is mentioned only as having been born and having entered the profession of mathematics. Nowhere is there again mention of him. We know he lived past the age of twenty-four because he was admitted to a profession. At that time, his parents had been married twenty-eight years. Statistics show that most females jump between the ages of thirty and thirty-six when it is marital dissolution that is the motive for suicide. So the chances are that she didn't jump because she couldn't understand her husband's ideas. It little mattered, since they had brought him, and thus her, international prestige. We must assumed that she committed suicide for another reason.

"What could Fairweather have done that caused his wife to commit suicide and the Church to bring excommunication proceedings against him? What could he have done that so created remorse that he would lick the boot that kicked him? What remorse could be so vast and so genuine as to be regarded as penitence by the Church, and thus permit Pope Leo to again open the doors of the Church to the repentant sinner?"

She got up from the sofa and walked away from him, turning to face him. "Logic guides me to only one choice— filicide. Fairweather murdered his own son. Remember, 'Summoning all my social grace, I mix the hemlock to your taste.' "

"Oh, Helix," he almost roared his protest, "you're reading personal motives into the most impersonal, universal mind that ever existed."

She shook her head. "You've erected a god in your mind. You believe Fairweather capable of nothing but divine behavior. I faced the possibility that the state could practice censorship. Match your courage with mine, and face the facts of logic."

"I can back you up with the information that Pope Leo was humanitarian," he said, "but logic will trip you. If Fairweather had murdered his own son, he would have been excommunicated."

"Not if there was legal doubt"—she stressed the word 'legal'— "which would have got him the support of Soc and Psych. They are concerned with legality, while the Church is concerned with morality. If he put piranhas in the swimming pool without telling his son. . . . you follow?"

"Yes," he agreed, "but Soc and Psych would not buck the church on mere legalities."

"Oh, wouldn't they?" she flashed. "What was the life of a half-breed prol to them? Nothing! What would the manner of his dying mean to the Church? Everything!

"Now, suppose Soc and Psych wheeled into line, not to protect Fairweather I so much as to oppose and crush the

Church. Suppose they hit on the Fairweather trial as a *cause célèbre*. What would they gain?"

So his father, with vaster knowledge than hers, had hinted. His interest keyed higher as she walked over and picked up the history book.

"I've marked the passage. Listen: 'In the conclave of February 1952, redistribution of authority gave the Church complete spiritual authority over those not professing the faith'—remember, there were still a few Buddhists and Pharisaic Jews back in the first half of the nineteenth-century—'and full police power was invested in the Department of Psychology while the judicial functions were delivered to the Department of Sociology.' That shift was probably the direct outgrowth of the Fairweather trial."

Haldane leaned back on the sofa. She had done a splendid job of analysis, but she was reasoning like a female, intuitively. She had set up a theory and then gone looking for the facts to support it, rather than let the facts set up the theory.

"Judged purely on the basis of his work," Haldane said, "Fairweather was a great humanitarian. Humanitarians don't murder."

"Humanitarian!" Helix moved over and sat on the ottoman before him, as if she were begging him to understand her attitude.

"As children, you and I were required to watch the arrival and departure of the Hell ships. Remember those horrible gray slugs dropping out of the sky. Remember those spacemen waddling toward the cameras, heavy-jawed and thick-bodied, like toads oozing out of the primordial slime.

"Remember the Gray Brothers in their cowls, keening their liturgies as they carried the living dead up the long gangway of that ship? Remember the thud as the last port clanged shut like the door of a tomb? Remember those happy moments of our childhood, Haldane?

"Those little exercises in conditioning by terror, those little television shows we had to watch even though we awoke screaming at night, those ships, those crews, all came from the brain of Fairweather. Do you call *that* humanitarian?"

"Helix," he said, "you're looking at this purely from the viewpoint of a sensitive girl who was frightened. Even as a boy, I was never afraid to look at those ships, because they weren't Hell ships to me. They were starships.

"Fairweather did not design them as prison transports. He gave them to mankind as a bridge to the stars, but the Weird Sisters, Soc, Psych, and the Church, called them back from the stars. When the executives withdrew the space probes, Fairweather did the only thing that he could do; he salvaged the ships and the remnants of their crews.

"Those repulsive spacemen are the blood brothers of your romantic poets.

"The *Acheron* and the *Styx,* jumping in time warp between us and Arcturus, are the legacy Fairweather left us. If we can ever again rise to the heights our forefathers reached, those ships will be waiting to take us to the stars."

"Haldane, you're a strange and wonderful boy, but you cannot be objective about Fairweather."

"I can be objective about anything. . . . I'll grant your thesis that Fairweather could have murdered his son. Can you match my objectivity?"

"Absolutely."

Slowly, he cornered her. "Can you look at your own death objectively?"

"As objectively as any male!"

"If I told you that I loved you and was willing to die for that love, would you, with your knowledge of lovers, concede my sincerity?"

"That was one of the tenets of the lover cult. I'll accept it in theory, but I would never casually ask you to do it."

"Are you unselfish?"

"I like to think so, but I'd never volunteer the information if I weren't."

Her answers had snared her in his trap of sophistry, and he sprung the trap. "To paraphrase you, I'm going to ask you to 'match your unselfishness with my unselfishness, for I'm going to volunteer to die for you, and I ask you to listen with your vaunted objectivity."

So he heard himself dispassionately outlining his plan to merge their categories and mate. For the first time, he detailed to her his mathematical theory of aesthetics as applied to literature, and from his opening sentence she caught the implications. He knew this, from the anxiety and sadness in her eyes. Though much of what he said was in mathematical terms, she listened with a focused and intent silence that told him she understood. Only once, when he was explaining the mathematical weights given to the parts of speech, did she interrupt with a question in a voice that rang hollowly in her throat.

"What weight did you give the nominative absolutes?"

He explained, and detailed the courses she must take for her master's degree and her Ph.D. in order to merge their categories in the new category. Then, after an hour and a half, he was finished.

She turned her eyes from his face and looked through the window at the bay, now brilliant from sunlight beaming through a rain-rinsed sky. "Dark, dark, in the blaze of noon!"

She turned to him in the sad resignation of surrender.

"I wanted to open a door for you, and one for me. I wanted to bring to this tired old planet its last bright-eyed love. I thought our love could flourish, just a little while, in the desert. But there was a tiger in the oasis.

"For a long time, the climate of earth has been growing colder for us poets. No wonder the flame that warmed us has died. Oh, I'm not completely innocent. I fanned your flame for its inspiration to me, and now I find that I'm burning, too.

"So do I turn from the ashes of my fathers and the temples of my gods? Yes, because I'm not a fool who starves her love only to feed her pride.

"And you. If you fail, you'll be exiled to Hell. If you succeed, a few more human beings are dehumanized."

"But if I succeed, you and I will live and die together."

"Since I love you to the depth and breadth and height

my soul can reach, this is not a decision for my reason to make. It's a matter of my being. I accept your offer."

He did not rise to give her a ceremonial kiss. He sagged back in the seat. The deed was done, the pact was pledged, and surrounding the inner core of his determination he felt an aura of farewell. He felt as Columbus must have felt as he sailed past the Pillars of Hercules, or as Ivanovna must have felt as the particolored globe of her native earth dwindled beneath her, a feeling of finality tinged with fear.

He lifted his face to Helix. "There is one fact I must know. Is it possible for the founder of a new category to define the genetic requirements? Logically, the answer is yes, but if the answer is no, we can curse God and die."

"How can you find out?"

"I can ask my father."

"If he suspects this plot, he'll issue a verbal edict," she warned, "and the world's last lovers never will have experienced the act of love."

When she made the remark, it was lost in the whirl and seethe of his thoughts, but later, as Christmas neared and his long separation from her during the holidays gave him more time to remember and to analyze her remarks, he read into her words a promise and a desire.

From her home in Sausalito, she sent his father a respectful Christmas card which let Haldane know of her thoughts. He himself, after buying the yearly offering of gin for his Father, was done with Christmas shopping. The week before Christmas and the week before New Year's were both spent in reading.

He read the complete works of John Milton because he remembered the venom in her phrase, "that unspeakable John Milton," and he wondered why the poet had aroused her contempt. He loved the sonorous phrases in the stilted language of that era, and he particularly admired the character of Lucifer in *Paradise Lost*. There was a man!

He knew, now, that such a work would be banned by the state, but it was written in an era before Lincoln had brought about the political hegemony of the United Nations. Long before any overtones of treason or deviation-ism could affix themselves to the poem, it had established itself as a classic, and Satan kept his status as the Prince of Darkness.

Reading further into Milton's works, he ran across the line, "Dark, dark, in the blaze of noon," and remembered that Helix had quoted it when she was under stress from his suggestion. He felt like calling her and asking, "If you detest the poet, why do you quote him?"

His relations with his father were very, very circum-spect. He was an astonishingly obedient and respectful son, playing chess constantly and losing ten percent of the time. Not until Sunday after New Year's Day, his last night at home, did he feel the time was right for him to cash a dividend on his exemplary behavior.

Over the chessboard, he asked, "Dad, do the geneticists ever cross-breed categories?"

"When the need develops. We were having trouble, some years back, with interplanetary navigators succumbing to space madness. They bred a female mathematician to a long-distance runner. His pulse beat was about half that of a normal man, and he had the nervous system of a turtle. The idea was to breed them to get a torpid mathe-matician. Three times they were bred, and each time the offspring was a nervous turtle. The dam got attached to her children and jumped when they put the last one to sleep, and the sire kept running."

Haldane studied the board and moved his knight.

He was in a position to checkmate in three moves, and he knew his father would see the pattern; but while his father was warding off the knight, the bishop, still in its original position, was the main threat.

As Haldane figured, his father moved into a defensive position to guard against the knight.

Haldane moved the bishop.

His father, desperately on the defensive, sought to counteract the bishop's move. Haldane, watching his fa-ther think, said, "Have you ever heard of a mating at the request of a professional himself?"

"Fairweather's the only one I ever heard of."

His father had brushed the question aside to concentrate on the board.

Haldane spoke again. "Suppose two members of a working team, in different categories, were particularly well-coordinated in their work effort. . . ."

"The sociologists would know it!"

"Would they recognize a petition from the team members?"

There was the question, put bluntly but camouflaged by casualness. The answer came maddeningly slowly, and it was incomplete. "Possibly. It would depend on the circumstances."

His father moved to counter the bishop. Haldane moved his knight and said, "Check!"

Haldane III wetted his lips and studied the board. There was a solution to his problem. He could sacrifice his castle and free his queen to check his son which would demand that his son sacrifice his knight.

Haldane waited for the flickering half-smile followed by a study of his son's alternatives. When it came, Haldane asked, "If an anthropologist were to run across some aspect of a primitive culture that he thought might throw light on present-day problems—that is, if his studies veered into the field of social anthropology—could he then petition the sociologists for a sociologist for his mate rather than another anthropologist?"

"Suppose! Suppose! What the hell you getting at?"

Haldane III's attention shifted from the chessboard to his son, his eyes blazing, a pallor suffusing his face.

"Christ, Dad, can't I ask a hypothetical question without your jumping on me with both feet?"

"Let me give your hypothetical question a hypothetical answer. If a genuine social need was evinced in such a petition, it would be considered. If there was the slightest ground for suspicion that such a petition was based on sexual attraction, a thorough study of both principals would be made with a view toward uncovering regressive tendencies. If a professional is found to be atavistic, he or she is reduced to the proletariat and sterilized by the order of the State.

"Any professional who brought such a petition might

61

well be writing his own death warrant. This danger would be doubled if the petition were for extracategorical breeding. It would be trebled if the proposed merger involved an art and a science. It would be a predetermined fact if the categories were mathematics and poetry!"

His father knew!

All the old antagonisms toward his father coiled in his mind, but caution stayed his hand.

Feigning casualness, he said, "That's a pretty specific answer to a hypothetical question."

"I don't like to see a man beat around the bush. Your mother thought I was an opinionated fool, but I was always honest. Now I'm going to give you a little honest paternal advice. Forget that girl Helix!"

"Why bring her into this?"

"Don't act so innocent! Did you truly think I wouldn't wonder why art and I started to get so much attention from you, especially after a Sappho with an abacus under her arm practically forced herself into my apartment? Epic poem of Fairweather—what a dodge!"

Sarcasm yielded to sincerity in his father's voice. "Listen, son. Those genetic laws protect us. Without them, every moony-eyed teen-aged frail would be spewing defective offspring from any passing sperm source who buttered her vanity. Their bastards would be up to our navels.

"The laws protect you. No amateur facility has the capabilities to produce a quality product at the price the pros charge, and when you go to the goat's house for wool, you *always* end up paying twice the price for shoddy.

"The laws protect me. I don't want to see a red X at the end of the line of Haldane merely because my son is an inept merchandiser on the frail market."

Haldane resented the sneering reference to his merchandising ability from a man who had tossed a diamond onto a five-and-dime counter. "You seem more proud of that line than of me!"

"Why not? You and I are just fractions in a continuum, but the name we bear means something."

"Maybe I don't want to be a cipher in a series. Maybe I'd like to be the sum of the digits."

"My god, what arrogance! If you were a child, I might sympathize with your prattle. If you have no regard for your dynasty, at least think of your own intellect. If you, by any act, deprive society of the services of that mind, you've committed a crime against humanity."

"If I have grave doubts about the worth of society, then anything I contribute to it is a sin against myself."

" 'Grave doubts about society'! Who are you to doubt society? You're only twenty. Are these the ideas you've been picking up from that frail?"

Haldane rose, his body tense, his face white. "Listen, old man, I'm tired of you calling her a frail."

"You want me to tell you what she is?"

Gently Haldane stepped back from the table. Carefully he placed his chair in its proper position. Almost gingerly he walked into the library and gathered his books into a neat pile. He secured the books tightly, forming a looped handle with the belt.

He got his cloak from the closet, took his books, and walked through the living room, toward the entrance.

His father rose and followed him to the door, asking, "Where are you going?"

"I'm getting out of here before I break your neck."

Haldane III was suddenly gentle.

"Listen, son. I apologize for my anger. I have no grievance against the girl except as a force acting on you. I enjoyed being the focus of her peculiar power, but she is not of us. She isn't old, I know, but she was never young. In your innocence, you've placed yourself under the sway of a Delilah.

"It isn't she that I'm concerned with, but you. You're my son, my only replacement. . . ."

"Dad, we're miles apart. Yes, I'm your replacement. After me comes Haldane V, stamped with the same parts number. We're parts in a computer! Fairweather's humanism was shown in his irony when he turned God into a solid-state computer.

"What's our purpose? Where are we going? After all, this is the best of all possible societies on the best of all possible planets."

"Don't you believe that?"

"Not any more."

Haldane III sat down on the sofa. A dazed look was on his face. "She did this to you."

"She did nothing. She asked questions, and I found the answers. Your society, the computing machine, has dehumanized everything, even the relationship between you and me. But Dad, I'm going to beat the machine. Fairweather did it, and so can I!"

"Sit down! I want to tell you something."

Despite his father's monotone, there was something burning in the voice that commanded obedience. Haldane sat down.

"You think Fairweather I was the last humanist. Pope Leo XXXV was the last humanist."

His father ceased speaking for a moment as if trying to gather his thoughts. His eyes focused on some distant object, and his breath came in rasps. "I'll tell you a state secret. Fairweather fathered a monstrosity by that proletarian mate, Fairweather II, a being who created more evil on this planet than any evil since the Starvation. Despite the evil of Fairweather II, Pope Leo brought excommunication proceedings against Fairweather I because he betrayed his own son to the police."

Again there was the silence marred by the breathing. Finally, he continued, "I want you to know this because if you are correct in your arrogance, if you are capable of duplicating his feats, I want you know what kind of model you have chosen.

"Pope Leo considered the betrayal a moral wrong. He brought charges against Fairweather on purely human grounds. The sociologists and psychologists argued that Fairweather I had put his social duty above his moral duty. They won. The pope lost. But Fairweather I sent his own son to Hell."

"How did you learn this?"

Suddenly the shards of Haldane III reassembled into the cold hauteur of the professional. "Are you questioning the knowledge of a department member, student?"

"I've earned the right to question such a charge against Fairweather, department member!"

"Get out!" Authority burned in every line of Haldane III's face.

Haldane grabbed his books and strode past him, but he turned in the doorway, sick with fury and despair.

There sat the destroyer, unbending, uncompromising, a gin-drinking, chess-playing, evil old man. He hated Helix. He hated his wife. He hated his son. Now he hated the memory of Fairweather!

With his brain churning, Haldane said, "Tell me, did my mother fall from that window, or did she jump?"

His father crumpled back onto the sofa. Pain replaced anger. He closed his eyes and waved his hand in a gesture of futility and defeat as Haldane slammed the door behind him.

Driving back to the campus, his anger left him, and as his rage subsided he knew that it had been the last tropical storm before an advancing ice age of his mind. The king was dead, destroyed by Haldane's sure knowledge that his father had spoken the truth, and Helix was a snow maiden lost in the frozen mists. Fairweather, that worse-than-filicide, was a pope-building sycophant of the Church.

He wanted to pray to something, but in the vast desolation only the ghosts of old gods snickered. Yet, even as he adjusted to this sub-subarctic of the spirit, an aurora borealis flickered and then flared into a dazzling display of rustling light which sent his blood singing through his veins.

$LV^2 = (-T)$

If he could prove that, he would need no gods to pray to!

Then the lights flickered out. It was true, and he knew it, but no laboratory on earth had the facilities to permit its demonstration.

His thoughts swung back to the ice field.

Chapter Six

HALDANE'S FIRST MONDAY LECTURE, ON STRESS ANALYSIS, bored him under ordinary conditions. Originally he had selected the dull subject with a boring lecturer as a buffer for his Monday morning aches. Now, fatigued from a sleepless night, he found it doubly difficult and doubly necessary to concentrate on unemotional facts lest the despair that skirted the periphery of his consciousness gain complete control.

That mighty edifice of thought which he had planned to erect in secret had been bared by the offhand deductions of his father. Now Helix would flee from him, leaving him nothing but his shattered self-esteem because the poetess had been right and the mathematician wrong about Fairweather. Then there were the shards of that shattered idol who had betrayed humanity in such a monstrous manner.

Above all, there was the memory of the pain on the face of his father. He didn't believe for a moment that his mother's death was suicide, but there would have been enough self-reproach from old family quarrels in his father's mind to give the accusation a cutting edge.

He was hardly seated when remorse gave way to anger.

"Dean Brack wants to see you, Haldane IV."

A messenger entered the class quietly and whispered the words in his ear.

Haldane gathered his books and stalked out of the class.

He was well aware that his father had not called the dean to warn him of his son's atavistic leanings. Such a call would have compromised his father.

Following the practice of department members, Haldane III was transferring his son to "broaden the scope of his studies." He was probably being reassigned to a metal-lurgy school on Venus.

Haldane himself had a few strings he could pull. He was in the top ten percent of his class, and Dean Brack would be loath to release a student who would drag down the overall average of the School of Mathematics. He would give the dean all the ammunition he needed to block his father's action.

Jaws clenched, body rigid, he strode into the dean's office, and the secretary waved him to the head of the line of waiting students. He was glad there would be little delay. He wanted to join battle immediately.

There was no point in revealing his aggressiveness to the dean. Before he passed through the doorway, his face was set in the impassive mask of the professional.

There was nothing impersonal about the dean.

"Sit down, Haldane," he said, very gently.

"Thank you, sir."

"Ordinarily, I open conversation with my students by inquiring about their grades, but your record is pleasantly known to me."

"Thank you, sir."

He spoke gropingly to Haldane. "Sometimes my duties are unpleasant . . . I . . . er . . . listen, boy, there's abso-lutely nothing I can say to make this pleasant. Last night, your well-beloved and talented father passed away."

"How?"

"Brain hemorrhage. He died in his sleep."

"Where is he? Where did they take him?"

"His body is being prepared at the Sutro mortuary. He'll be given a state funeral tomorrow, at the Cathedral of Saint Gauss. Of course, you're excused from your studies for the remainder of the week."

Compassion was in the silence that the dean let fall. Finally, he suggested, "If you need the consolation of our faith, the chapel is open."

Haldane did not desire the consolation of faith, but the dean's suggestion acted on his mind as a command as he left the office in a daze and walked across the campus toward the chapel.

Inside the chapel was cool and dark. He genuflected

and knelt in a pew near the altar above which loomed the Crossbow.

He tried to think of the agony of Christ in His final assault against Rome, but Christ had died at the height of His final victory, a meaningful death at the hands of the enemies of the Church. The arrow had not been driven into His chest by His son.

Yet, when he left the chapel, he felt more at peace. It had given him a dark place into which he could crawl and lick his wounds.

Back in his room, he lay down and let the long day rasp through him.

Later, Malcolm came and offered condolences. As the telecasts spread the news of the death, other students entered to pay their respects. As long as they were talking to him, he was not alone with his thoughts. He dreaded the coming night with its solitude.

Malcolm offered to drive him to the funeral, and he accepted.

When he and Malcolm arrived at the Stockton Street cathedral, it was crowded and oppressive with the odor of flowers. Most of the audience was of the professional class which had known his father, but there was a sprinkling of proletarians come to see a corpse which would be buried.

Haldane was oblivious to them all as he and Malcolm were ushered in to wait. Shortly after he was seated, he felt the pressure of a hand on his own and turned to find that Helix had seated herself beside him. She was not weeping, but her eyes were sad.

Helix awakened his awareness, and he noticed other females in the audience, some openly dabbing their eyes with handkerchiefs. In strange juxtaposition to his grief came the thought that his father had moved, perhaps, in areas that his son was not aware of.

Though the idea bemused him, it brought no consolation, no more than the flowers, the friends, and the eventual intonations of the priest sounding the sacraments men had used for ages to cheat despair.

He noticed, as he led the procession to view the remains

of the departed, that there was a trace of a smile on the face of the corpse. It was the beginning of the smile, slightly sardonic and wholly amused, he had seen a thousand times on his father's face as he raised his face from the chessboard after a move which had trapped his son.

Once in the open sunlight, in the clean, bright air, Haldane stiffened and his grief became encased in formality. "Helix, may I present Malcolm III, my roommate?"

Turning to Malcolm, he said, "Helix knew Father."

"Always glad to meet a poet," Malcolm said, noticing the A-7 stitched on her tunic. "Can't help turning a page, now and then. I know a trochee from an anapest. So you knew his father. I never met him."

"He was an adorable man," Helix said, using functional language to fill the silence. "His death was a loss to society."

"Let's all go have a cup of coffee," Haldane suggested.

"Can't." Malcolm demurred. "Got a quiz this afternoon and I'm crammed for it. I've got to get back before I slosh over. Glad to have met you, Helix."

With a wave of his hand, Malcolm was gone.

"Wasn't he driving you back?" Helix asked.

"I have the week off."

"He's the boy whose parents own the apartment, isn't he?"

"Yes."

"Did he know about us?"

"Of course not. . . . I mentioned you when I met you at Point Sur, but he's forgotten. . . . Look, Helix. Dad knew about us."

"How could he?"

"He reasoned his way to the knowledge."

Sudden fear crossed her features. "I'll go back to classes. You go and pack your belongings. Don't spend the night in your dad's apartment; it'll depress you. Take a hotel."

"I can't worry about safety," he said. "I must talk to you. Meet me at the apartment."

Almost whispering, she said, "If you need me, I have no choice. I'll be there."

69

Watching her go, he felt primitively alone among the press of mourners emerging from the cathedral, acknowledging the occasional pat on the back, the pressure of a hand on his arm, or a murmured, "I'm sorry."

Helix was waiting when he arrived at the apartment. She took him by the hand and led him to the sofa where he blurted out, "Helix, I killed my father."

"Nonsense. The newscasts said he died of a brain stroke."

"I caused it."

"Oh, no," she said.

Haltingly at first, and then rapidly, Haldane poured out the story of his argument with his father. She listened in silence as he spoke, piling detail onto detail, sparing her nothing. "When I hit him with that blow about Mother's death, that killed him."

"You were both angry. You were no more to blame than he."

"It was up to me to keep the conversation calm. I was the supplicant, the son. He might have had a change of heart, helped us. Not once did he issue an edict forbidding our meetings. And you had aroused his primitivism, so he knew its power.

"If he had thrown Mother out the window, he would have been no more reprehensible than I, because I poured his hemlock."

"You've got to quit saying that, and you've got to quit believing it." Her voice rang with certainty. "It isn't true. You had a family argument, in anger but not in hatred. You told him, by implication, that you intended to commit a crime against the state. Did you expect him to shout with glee? Of course not, silly! He was shocked, and the shock contributed to his already weakened condition. Your scorn didn't kill him. His love for you killed him, and it was an accident."

"I'm tired," he said. "Bone tired."

Somehow, her words dulled the edge of his guilt, and he felt, suddenly, as if he had gone an eternity without sleep.

"Stretch out, Haldane. Here, pillow your head on my lap."

As she stroked his hair, he said, "I did love him. And I love you. Yet, if one love must cancel the other, I prefer his canceled, because without you. . . . They said he died in his sleep. I don't accept that. That stroke must have plowed through his brain like a sledge hammer. . . . But it was a gentle tap compared to the blow I struck. . . ."

She let him ramble on, talking not as a man but as a stricken child with all defenses down.

His confessional eased him, and he was drifting into sleep when the memory of his father's face floated into his mind. He saw it contorted with pain, and his body stiffened as he moaned, "I should have died."

She took his handkerchief and wiped his forehead, crooning to him, "Dear boy, dear boy. . . ." The tension in her voice fought against the resurgent wave of guilt that was threatening his mind, and she cuddled his head as if to shelter it from the internal storm.

He felt it when she ceased to stroke his hair, but his eyes were closed and he did not see the deft movement of her free hand as she unbuttoned her tunic. He sensed her bending lower, coming closer, and felt the gentle wedging apart of his lips as she crooned, "Here, my infant, my nursling, feed on life!"

So it was that he came to know her in primitive simplicity and beauty, and the knowledge of her was like nothing he had ever known or ever imagined that he could know.

Next day he resumed his classes.

Grief stayed with him for a long while, but the remorse had been replaced by regret. It was as if the actions of Helix explained and justified the death of his father.

There were four months left to them before the Malcolms returned, and he and Helix accepted the time remaining as they had taken that dark-bright Tuesday. For him there was no satiety, and they revived and relived the old endearments of romance. They were sweethearts, and they used the term.

Even when all passion was cleanly spent, he still de-

71

lighted in talking to her, touching her, and watching the secret lights of her being flash into view.

There could be an acid to her flavor.

Once, as he complimented her on purely technical matters, she said, "Someone has to take the initiative, my darling. If I hadn't taken advantage of your grief and seduced you, we'd still be sitting on the sofa holding hands."

He questioned her dislike of John Milton. "I don't care for the tone of moral indignation that he uses. Now and then, a sin justifies itself, and there's always an argument for the devil. That man was a statist before there was a state. He's no more than an apologist for the sociologists."

Time seemed to rush toward their last Saturday together.

On the first Saturday in April, with three more to go, he arrived at the apartment to find her there before him. Usually, he arrived first to dust, check for microphones, and bring the flowers which had become so important to the spirit they had recreated.

Outside it was misting rain from intermittent squalls, and she stood moodily by the window and let him arrange the flowers alone.

He could understand the moodiness. He shared it. They had taken down a calendar visible from the living room on the kitchen wall, and agreed not to mention time.

Finished with the flowers, he walked up behind her, put his arms around her, and said, "Now I know what that silly little ditty meant by 'the rack of time's compressing.' "

There were tears in her eyes. She put her arm around him and almost wearily walked with him back to the sofa.

"Granted, dear, that we have only three more days left, we can't spend it sitting like two old people, huddling together against the storms of mortality."

Instead of turning to him with her old ardor, she merely took his hand in hers and continued to gaze at the window.

Suddenly she spoke, and there was infinite sadness in

her voice: " 'Now that you're tortured on the rack of time's compressing, I'll murder you, beloved, as my final blessing.' Haldane, I'm pregnant."

"My god!" The arm he was placing around her went suddenly limp and fell to his side.

He felt the physical presence of the state.

It was one thing to joust with dragons on some far-off tilting day when his lance was honed and he was mounted and mailed. It was another, lanceless and without armor, to find the dragon coiled within this room and breathing flames.

She was trapped. This girl of tender flesh and fragile bones carried with her the evidence of a conspiracy that would destroy them both.

"Are you sure?"

"I'm sure."

He got up and paced the floor. "There are drugs."

"Ask for them at the pharmacy and you'll be arrested on the spot."

"Who was that Frenchman, Thoreau, who had the idea that running around on all fours would make a miscarriage come about?"

"It was Rousseau," she said, "and it was to make childbirth easier."

"If we could get you into a centrifuge."

"Not unless you're going to another planet."

He sat down on the sofa, breathing heavily. "Maybe a trampoline. . . ."

"What would a professional be doing acting like a circus prol?"

He thought for a moment. She could take a trip out to Sea Lion Park and ride the roller-coaster. She could tilt her body back to get the true perpendicular to the uterus. . . .

"I think," he said, noticing for the first time that if the brocaded tiger were to lunge forward, it would not strike the nose of the elongated roebuck head that formed the base of the end lamp. It would claw the roebuck's eye.

"What do you think?"

"I think anything we say or do is academic." He got up and walked over to the end lamp, lifting it. Beneath the hollow base of the end lamp, lying on the table, was a small metallic object no larger than a tarantula but far more deadly. All the sounds they had made had been picked up and broadcast to a distant amplifier.

Where were the listeners? A block away? Half a block away? In this very building?

Whoever listened heard the end lamp lifted. They heard his hand wrap itself around the microphone as he carried it to a side window, and they heard the crunch as it landed on the pavement eight stories below.

"You shouldn't have destroyed it," she said. "Now you'll be charged with destroying state property. They'll make you regret and repent."

Shaken by waves of anger and fear that canceled each other, he stood before her, outwardly unshaken, preparing his last will and testament for the only being he loved.

He sensed that in her present turmoil she would little note nor long remember what he said here unless he could associate his words with phrases she knew already and would never forget. So, to preserve for her, forever, a reminder of his love, his genius of desperate inspiration leaped to his side, and he said, "Regret a microphone? No! Not for that, nor what the pimps of Soc and Psych may else inflict do I repent or change, but will always feel a high disdain for those unthinking shepherds who overwhelm us with their stench of lanolin."

"But, what can we do, Haldane?"

"Beloved, I know not what course you may take but as for me, I'll fight. I'll fight them here, I'll fight them in the slimes of Venus, I'll fight them, if need be, from the frozen corners of Hell. I'll never surrender!

"I'm not the master of my fate, but I'm the captain of my mind, and I shall not cease from mental strife, nor shall my thoughts sleep in my brain, till we have built anew upon this earth an edifice of liberty . . ."—his voice sank—". . . or death."

He sat down beside her, his face white with anger, breathing in short gasps, catching in an open palm the vicious punches of his fist.

Her keen mind grasped his intentions. Leaning over to stroke his hair, she said, "So fair, so bright!" Then she spoke to him, saying, "I cannot change the tenor of your thoughts nor make our coming trials a little thing, but if I could raise my hand and say to the evidence within me, 'Out, damned spot,' my heart would still cry 'Hold!', for this, my hand, would rather, a layette weave of star beams, making the dim rays bright.

"Oh, I would have made you coffee and brioches for your delight, and tea for you at tea-time, with cocoa at night. When I am far away, remember me a little."

Her voice broke, and she could speak no more.

His own voice was breaking, but he forced it to carry on. Turning to her, he said, "Remember! I'll always remember this April as laughing through tear-drenched eyes, because you came to me with accents sweet in the dark night of our souls. But this night is such stuff as dreams are made on, and knowing you will round that night, for me, with a death of pleasant sleep.

"You'll trip always through my heart in your light, fantastic manner, stay always buxom, blithe, and debonair, for you are the queen among women, Helix, who lay by my side. As my thoughts' companion, you will never grow old."

Wildly they clung, composing a shorthand of mumbled phrases which would give their lives, via connotations, an old age of companionship which the state had now, forever, denied.

For the two policemen and the policewoman who walked into the room, their language might have sounded like the cooing of demented doves.

Chapter Seven

THE EMBARCADERO STATION WAS ALMOST DESERTED when the policemen brought in Haldane. It was too early in the afternoon for the run of Saturday drunks, but the place reeked of their past presence. A flunky was swabbing the floor with a mop dipped in a disinfectant which overpowered the stench with a fouler odor. The only other civilian present was a lanky man in a trenchcoat, his feet propped up on the bench he sat on to avoid the swishing mop. He was intent on a pocket novel.

"Got one for you, Sergeant," one of the arresting officers said to the booking officer who sat behind a desk.

"Name and gene des," the booking sergeant asked, looking at Haldane with the cold, impersonal gaze the professional usually reserves for the proletarian.

Haldane, wearing his own mask, answered.

"What's the charge, Frawley?" the sergeant asked the policeman.

"Miscegenation and impregnation, suspicion of. We took the frail to the medical O.D. uptown. Her report should be back from the office by midnight."

"Put him in storage," the sergeant said, "and make out the report."

"Just a minute, Sergeant." The lanky civilian unfolded from the bench and walked over to join them. "May I have a word with the prisoner?"

"Sure, Henrick," the sergeant said, "he's public property."

Henrick, the civilian, took a note pad and the stub of a pencil out of his pocket. His movement revealed a tunic. Barely legible under beer or gravy stains, Haldane could read the designation of Communicator, class 4.

He was thin, florid-faced, red-haired, and freckled. His Adam's apple protruded obnoxiously. A hint of spittle clustered in the corners of his thin lips, and the odor of whisky coming from his mouth made the odor of the disinfectant mild in comparison. If he had been a dog, the shape of his droopy blue eyes would have put him in the cocker spaniel breed. But he was not a dog; he was a newspaper reporter.

"My name's Henrick. I work for the *Observer*."

His announcement held a fatuous note, as if he were pleased with himself for being connected with the newspaper.

Haldane said, "So?"

76

"I heard your name and gene des. There was another M-5, Haldane, who died about the second or third of January this year. If I remember, he was III. That would make you his son, right?"

"Yes."

"Too bad he's dead. He might have helped you. Would you mind giving me the name and the gene des of the female?"

"Why should I?"

"I don't want to work overtime. I want to get home. I can get it off the booking desk but it'll be midnight before it's down from uptown. If you don't tell me, I'll have to wait around. We don't get many professionals through here. Very few on impregnation charges, so this is a big story."

Haldane remained silent.

"There's a bigger reason," Henrick continued. "I'm a feature writer, not an ordinary leg man sending in reports to the rewrite desk. Whatever way I run the story, that's the way it's printed. I can slant it one of two ways. I can play you up as as a thinker too stupid to use protection, and that'll give the prols a big charge. They like to see a professional make a fool of himself.

"On the other hand, I can play you up as a gambling man, a good old down-to-earth human being who got a yen for a frail and said, 'To hell with shaking hands with gloves on!' That'll make you a hero to the prols."

"What do I care what the proletarians think?"

"You don't care now. In another fortnight or so, it will make a difference. You'll be down there with them."

Haldane was struck by the man's logic as well as his diffident manner. Here was a C-4, a category admitted to the professions less than a decade ago, whose lot could not be a happy one. Day after day he sat in police stations, watching the rejects of humanity pass and trying to weave from the warp and woof a tapestry with a little color, if not of beauty then of "human interest."

No doubt Henrick sympathized with the flotsam he encountered, for the odor of whisky that floated around him was a symptom of tensions.

Thinking of the man before him not as the symbol of

77

all reporters but as an individual with unique problems, carrying his pride as a defense against the reality of his work and shoring that pride, when it faltered, with alcohol, Haldane felt for the first time in his life a compassion for a personality with which he was not familiar.

Dropping his mask, Haldane asked gently, "Henrick, why do you want to get home?"

"My mate. She isn't much, but she worries about me. She thinks I drink too much. Today is her birthday, and I wanted to give her a surprise by being home for dinner."

"Henrick, I don't want you to keep your mate waiting on her birthday."

Haldane gave him the name and genealogical designation of Helix. "Treat the girl kindly in your story. Gentleness was her only crime, so be gentle with her."

Informality between professionals at their first meeting was gauche, and a request for sympathy, even for a third party, skirted the edge of sentimentality and familiarity. Haldane intended no plea, but he had sensed a secret misery in the gaunt man with the red hair.

His own compassion sought and found compassion. Henrick reached out and grasped his hand, "Good luck, Haldane."

Not only did Henrick grasp his hand, but when Haldane glanced up he noticed the coldness had gone from the desk sergeant's eyes. Frawley, the policeman, took his arm and said, almost gently, "This way, Haldane."

Frawley led him down a corridor to a cell, unlocked it, and led him in. It was a room with wallpaper, a bunk, a chair, and a table with a Bible on it. Except for the bars on the window, it could have been a hotel room.

Haldane turned to Frawley. "How did you know we were in that apartment?"

"Your friend, Malcolm, tipped us off. You were using the place with his permission, and he thought he might be picked up as an accessory. I shouldn't be telling you this, but you seem different from the other professionals. You almost act like a prol."

With the dubious compliment of the policeman ringing

in his ears, Haldane sat on the edge of the bunk and removed his shoes.

Out of the tragedy of his arrest, two things had taken place which heartened him. One had happened in the booking office, when his own humanity had established a bridge, however tenuous, with other human beings.

The other incident had occurred in the apartment when the policewoman had taken Helix away. As he had taken his last earthly look at the face of the girl he loved, he had read the expression on her face, and there had been no terror or anxiety in her eyes. Instead, he had seen pride and a form of exultation, as if she considered her lover a saint and gloried in sharing his martyrdom.

That night he lay down to the soundest sleep he had slept in months, and he arose refreshed to take delight in breakfast.

He knew he had come to the Second Ice Age of his mind, but he was getting acclimated to the cold. His sensibilities were frozen and all of his problems were the problems of a corpse. Despair without hope was an anodyne to pain.

An hour after breakfast, the door of his cell blew inward from the cheerful gust of a fresh breeze, bearing a briefcase, in the form of a smiling young man with blond hair who stuck out a hand in greeting, saying, "I'm Flaxon I, your attorney."

As Haldane rose to shake his right hand, he tossed the briefcase on the table, slid the table aside with his free hand, and hooked his foot under the leg of the chair to bring it facing Haldane's bunk. He was seating himself in the chair facing Haldane before Haldane had resumed his seat on the edge of the bunk.

He had not wasted a single motion. Verily, Haldane concluded, this man was the most efficient he had ever seen.

"Before we get down to business, I'll introduce myself. You don't have to. I was up at four, this morning, reading the police report and your dossier. You're the only professional I've ever been assigned to. We don't get many in this court.

"I'm the first Flaxon. My father was a San Diego law

clerk, and, when I showed an aptitude for the law, the state gave me a break. I took a competitive exam at USC and was third in a class of 542. You're looking at the head of a dynasty."

Haldane greeted Flaxon's biography with a sheepish grin. "From one going down to one coming up, greetings."

"Wrong remark, Haldane." Flaxon's smile changed to a look of gravity. "Why? It shows flippant humor about a serious situation which, in turn, reflects an indifference to your social position. You fellows in the categories for two or three generations tend to take your responsibilities to the state far too lightly.

"We owe it to the state to be in their hitting on every play of the game. Right here, in this district, there are judges who spend more time on tennis courts than in law courts.

"Take you. Prime example! With all the houses the state provides students for recreation, you invade another category and, Hell's cold, you don't even use a contraceptive. And she didn't! You two were *trying* to get caught!"

"They know for sure she is pregnant?"

"Of course. You're charged with impregnation."

"Have you seen Helix or talked to her?"

"I have no reason to see her. I'm defending you. Why worry about her, anyway?

"Now, you're guilty as charged. No doubt about it, because the impregnation proves the miscegnation, a misdemeanor proves a felony—if that isn't moving a mountain with a crow bar!

"In a week or ten days, depending on the docket, you'll be tried and sentenced. Before trial, you'll be interviewed by the jurors: a sociologist, a psychologist, and a priest. There is a fourth chosen from the category of the defendant, in this case a mathematician.

"Our task is to influence that jury."

"But, Flaxon, why worry about the jury, or the judge either, if it's a foregone conclusion that I'm guilty?"

"Good question. Shows you're thinking. Answer: our plea will be for clemency.

"As we say in law, there are stratifications to declassification. Granted you'll be sterilized and relegated to the prols, clemency may mean the difference between a soft berth on earth or the uranium mines of Pluto. So, the stakes are high.

"My plan for your defense has two approaches. First, we present all mitigating factors we can discover to temper the judgment of the court. Second, and most important, I intend to create such a favorable impression of you with the jurors that *they'll* be begging the judge to grant you clemency.

"First there are some questions I would like to ask, and one from sheer curiosity coupled with the hope that it might be important: why in the hell didn't you use a contraceptive?"

In answer, and picking up the tempo from his lawyer, Haldane rapidly summarized the events surrounding his father's funeral. "We just didn't come prepared," he explained lamely.

"Good!" Flaxon's voice was crackling with excitement. "That answer is important. You were overcome by grief. You turned to the girl for consolation. There was no plot to subvert the state's genetic laws.

"According to the deposition of your roommate, Malcolm, you and the girl met at the funeral. Since she was at your father's funeral, she was devoted to your father. You two turned to each other for comfort and consolation in the throes of your great grief."

"Flaxon, I hate to throw a discordant note into your approach, but it didn't happen like that. I was in a state of shock over dad's death, and Helix acted more to comfort me than from any mutual grief."

"The truth of situations is not inherent in the situations, but in the point of view taken by the viewer. You say her behavior was prompted more from concern for you than from mutual grief. I infer that it was prompted by the situation outside of yourselves. My point of view is correct for the trial.

"We want to keep the act that led to conception in the nature of an accident," Flaxon explained. "We play down any attraction between you two, because the degree of that attraction is the degree of your primitivism. We want sanitized sex.

"We can account for subsequent assignations on the theory that you had found something new, different, and refreshing. The girl was not a pro, so we can assume she was a delightful change from the state house fare. . . . Hey, wait a minute!"

Flaxon's pell-mell rush skidded to a halt. "When did your father die?"

"January third."

"But she's only one month pregnant, and it's April! What the hell! Who was in charge of the security detail in that arrangement? You or she?"

"She was. It seemed less . . . indelicate that way."

"Lord, did she muff her assignment! If she weren't killing herself in the act, I'd swear she was trying to hang you. . . . Well, our story stands, except the element of gross stupidity has been offered in addition to the element of grief. On the surface, you two were intellectually incapable of betraying the state. . . . Maybe that's a point in our favor."

Flaxon seemed hardly aware of his client as he leaned back, considering a defense in all honesty which rankled Haldane almost as much as the charges, but it was true.

He had not even thought about the time lapse until this moment.

Suddenly Flaxon's body became rigid, and he leaned forward. His eyes bored into Haldane's. "Now for the hundred credit question. Why did you throw that microphone out of the window?"

"I felt the police had heard enough. There was little point in broadcasting my last will and testament, since I wasn't leaving any heirs."

"You're rationalizing after a fact," Flaxon said bluntly. "Now, tell me the truth! Why did you throw that microphone out of the window?"

"All right, I was angry. It was a spontaneous thing. I did it without thinking."

"We're getting closer to the truth. It may be a bad truth, but we've got to find it if we wish to shape it in our direction. So, give me another answer: why did you throw that microphone out of the window?"

"I hated it!"

"But it was an inanimate object. How can you hate an inanimate object?"

"I hated what it represented."

"Now, we're getting down to bedrock. You hated it because it represented the power of the state. By extension, you hate the state. This is a bad truth.

"Throwing that microphone out of the window could be the worst thing you did in a series of acts, not one of which would have won you a good conduct medal from the Department of Sociology."

"You're reading too much into an impulse," Haldane said.

"*I'm* reading nothing; I'm only concerned with what your psychologist juror will think. Psychologists don't think as you and I. They think in a series of mental quirks hung loosely together by indefinite conjunctions.

"You could be guilty of the mass insemination of forty different categories by forcible assault, and if you kept rubbing your hands together, the psychologist would cease to wonder about your procreative crimes and hone in on the hands. He would build your scaffold out of *that,* for Christ's sake!

"I tell you, the microphone is bad, but we'll think about it."

Flaxon slapped his hands together as if to put a period to that troubling line of thought, rose, and walked over to the window. He looked out for a moment.

He turned suddenly, came back to the bunk, and sat down.

"I think there's a pattern here, something we can make attractive, but I'll need much, much more." He leaned back for a moment, reflecting, then turned again to Haldane.

"I want to give you a project. Write out for me every detail that happened between you and the girl from the first meeting. Don't justify. Don't explain. Leave that up to me, but tell the truth, even when it hurts.

"You can tell me anything. I'll make myself your alter ego and I'll explain the acts.

83

"What you tell me is absolutely privileged. As I read the notes, I'll burn them. By the time I'm through here, you'll know I'll never betray your confidence, like that rat, Malcolm, for if I did and they sent you to Pluto, you as a prisoner would have me dangling by the same item of anatomy that brought you here.

"I've got the paper in my brief case. You can start after I leave. My object is to learn enough about you to project your personality and character with sympathy. On the degree of sympathy we can arouse in the jurors depends the degree of clemency granted by the judge."

He leaned back on the bunk, resting on one elbow.

"Among the jurors, you won't have to worry too much about the mathematician. He'll be the custodian of your skills, sort of a job placement expert. He'll be your concern since he'll be evaluating abilities that I can't judge. But the priest. . . ."

He threw himself onto his feet, slapped his hands together, and walked again to the window.

"The priest won't like it that you turned to another human being for consolation. In matters touching on human mortality, one is expected to turn to the Church for consolation. In essence, you substituted a human female for Our Holy Mother. Incidentally, are you religious?"

"No."

"Did you have any religious thoughts when they told you your father was dead."

"I went to the chapel on the campus."

"Very good. That's better than a thought! Did you pray?"

"I knelt before the altar, but I couldn't pray."

"Good!"

Flaxon turned and began to pace back and forth the length of the cell. Haldane noticed that even his random movements were not without efficiency. He took the five maximum steps the space permitted, wheeled, and took five back. As he walked, he talked.

"Here's where we begin to sculpture the truth. Make it a point to tell the priest that you went to the chapel and knelt before the altar. He'll assume that you prayed, and we're not responsible for his assumptions.

84

"Perhaps you did pray. Didn't you even mumble a Pater Noster or count a bead or two?"

"No, I tried to sympathize with Christ. I finally decided that I couldn't because he had asked for it, and I hadn't."

"Don't tell him that! You're giving yourself a bosom-buddy relationship with Our Blessed Savior, and the Church loves humility, not only before God but before his representatives on earth.

"Keep that Bible open whether you read it or not, and don't open it to the Song of Solomon."

Flaxon walked over and drew a sheaf of notepaper from his folio. "Here's writing material. We'll have about five days before your interviews with the jurors, but I can get a continuance if we need it.

"I think we're lucky that there was a conception. Otherwise, you'd have been psychoanalyzed for sure, and something tells me that psychoanalysis would have meant Pluto for you. Now that primitivism is an established fact, we can present our picture rather than let the psychologists present theirs. Incidentally, have you ever undergone civilian analysis?"

"Once, when I was a child."

"What for?"

"Aggressions. I shoved some flower pots off a window sill and almost hit a pedestrian. My mother had fallen out of the window while watering the pots, and I blamed them."

Flaxon clapped his hands and flashed a broad grin. "That'll take care of the microphone!"

"How?"

"When you threw that microphone out of the window you were regressing to compulsive infantile behavior. Helix was your mother substitute. The microphone which destroyed her was the flower pots which destroyed your mother. You were reliving an old trauma."

"That theory sounds farfetched to me."

"That's the beauty of it. Listen," Flaxon leaned forward, his intensity compelling attention, "when the psychologist comes in, you say conversationally, 'This isn't the first time I've met your profession.'

"Naturally, he's going to ask for details, and you give them. Let him draw his own conclusions. You and I will have nothing to do with those conclusions."

He pulled out a handkerchief and wiped his brow. "Whew, I was worried about that microphone."

Haldane knew that Flaxon had been truly worried, and it moved him that a man whom he had known for less than an hour could become so involved in his problems. He was aware that lawyers were expected to defend their clients, but he was grateful that the state had assigned him a man so completely committed to his cause that he had called Malcolm a rat for fulfilling his duties as a citizen.

"Now, the sociologist is the jury foreman," Flaxon continued. "His duties are administrative, which means the other jurors make the decisions and he gets credit. Frequently he'll come up with a minor idea phrased in major language. His sentences will be so long that you'll forget the subject before he reaches the predicate, but pay him close attention, and I mean close.

"If you think he's trying to be witty, smile. If you know he's trying to be witty, laugh. He's a member of the ranking department, so curry his favor.

"In general, remember you're a professional and you'll be treated as one until you're sentenced. Be friendly, be casual, be frank, but *don't volunteer any information*. They've got facts enough to work on without our contributions."

Flaxon walked over to the window and looking out, said, "We've got some things going for us. You're intelligent, personable, and the affair started during an extreme emotional crisis. We've got to convince them that your delinquency did not spring from atavism."

He turned back and looked at Haldane, almost accusingly. "Frankly, from your interest in the girl, I think maybe you are a throwback, but that's all right with me." He grinned. "I've got a few atavistic tendencies myself.

"Get cracking on those notes. I'll be back in the morning to pick up what you've written. Remember, the more facts you can give me, the easier it will be for us to pick out the truths we can use in projecting an image of you as a noble, law-abiding lad."

There was a quick extension of the hand, a rapid shake, and Flaxon was slamming the door behind him.

Haldane shuffled the sheets of paper together as he turned to his task. He was constantly being surprised to find acute intelligences in mediocre professions. Within the limits of social orthodoxy, Flaxon had a mind that flashed and sparkled, was capable of profound insights, and was backed by human sympathies.

He liked the man. All during the interview, Flaxon had smiled, frowned, or grown pensive. Not once had he worn the mask.

Haldane began to write in straight, chronological order all the incidents that had occurred between the meeting at Point Sur and his arrest. He was writing at lunch time and writing when they brought supper. When he ran out of paper, he went to bed.

In the morning, he greeted Flaxon with, "Counselor, I need more paper."

Flaxon had come prepared. He pulled a sheaf from his briefcase, commented on the legibility of Haldane's handwriting, and left with the completed portion of the manuscript.

Fully committed to his task, Haldane relived every moment of his life with Helix. His principle aim in the composition was clarity, but he found that when he was describing his remembered passions, somehow a shadow of his emotion fretted through his words. As the work progressed, he knew he was writing for an audience of one the last love story on earth.

Flaxon must have spent more time analyzing the notes than Haldane did writing them. In the morning he would arrive haggard and tired, although his appearance was belied by his driving energy.

"About the epic poem of Fairweather," he would remark, "don't tell the priest you dropped it because you figured you couldn't get it published. Tell him you stopped the project after you found out the biography was proscribed. That is exactly what happened, and he will assume the religious motivation."

Then he might say, in one of those purely personal asides that endeared him to Haldane, "Don't go into details about your mathematics of aesthetics with the mathematician. For all I know, the idea is valid and you might want to work on it as a prol. Tip him on the idea, and twenty years from now you might find someone else's name appended to your theory."

He would badger the same idea from different angles. "Tell the sociologist about your theory. He'd like the social thinking behind your attempt to absorb an art category.

"Hit the psychologist with it, too. He'll be convinced that if you were working *that* kind of a deal with the girl, your relationship had to be on the plane of the superego. Your id slipped in when you weren't looking."

Flaxon's mind was constantly probing the material he got from the manuscript. "Don't let the sociologist know that you never feared the Hell ships. Those boys have spent time, energy, and credits conditioning you to feel terror. They don't take kindly to defeat."

Once he dropped a personal remark that spread ripples through Haldane's mind. "With your knowledge of Fairweather mechanics, you'd make a good engine room mechanic on a starship. There wouldn't be any competition for the job."

Despite the growing friendship between them, Flaxon would make no inquiries about Helix. "If I asked, they'd know where the inquiry came from, and you'd be prejudiced. Besides, her punishment will be gauged to yours, only lighter. Females are never regarded as aggressors in miscegenation cases, the point of law being that she has no point."

Each day, for two hours, Flaxon would go over the notes he had prepared from Haldane's manuscript, coaching his client.

"Now, about the girl. In reading about her, I was touched. No doubt your portrait of her is true. It is certainly beautiful, it may be prejudiced, and it's atavistic. You've succeeded in doing with her in my eyes what I hope to do with you in the jury's eyes.

"So, I'll warn you. Never hint to the jury that you felt for her anything more than transient desire. This they will understand. More than this they will understand, too, but not to our benefit."

88

Flaxon was giving to empty nothing the habitation and name of Haldane IV.

Without altering the basic facts, Flaxon was sculpting an image that would make Haldane appear to the priest as a young man of strong religious convictions, to the mathematician a brilliant but orthodox mathematician, to the sociologist a socially alive young fellow who had wished to eliminate a troublesome category, and to the psychologist a normal superego that had toppled before a superb libido.

At the end of five days, he and Flaxon agreed, after rehearsals, that the leading man was ready for his entrance.

"Tomorrow, you'll be interviewed," Flaxon said. "I'll burn your manuscript tonight and check with you tomorrow afternoon to see how the interviews came out. You take care of the jury, and I'll take care of the judge. Mine's the easy part."

They shook hands, and later, stretched on his bunk, Haldane felt the first feeling of confidence he had known for months. Whatever degree of clemency was granted him, he knew that Flaxon would get the highest for him that any lawyer could get, and he was not seeking the highest level of clemency; he intended to choose the lowest job on the priority scale.

In that First Ice Age of his discontent, he had discerned the incompleteness of Fairweather's Simultaneity Formula, $2(LV) = S$. But he had shoved that discovery behind him for his mortal affairs were pressing, and he knew that no laboratory on earth could offer him facilities to test the Haldane Theory, $LV^2 = (-T)$. But there was a laboratory, not of this earth, now available.

He might have believed that some divinity had shaped him to this end, had he not come to the conclusion that the mills which ground were not the gods'.

$LV^2 = (-T)$ would remove the stain of his father's blood, wipe out the damned spot which condemned him, and topple the Weird Sisters!

The Church was going to be gratified to receive into its arms the most penitent miscegenationist since the founding of the Holy Israel Empire, and the campus friends of

Haldane O, née IV, were going to be dumfounded to discover that the erstwhile Paul Bunyan of the recreational parlors had chosen the celibate life of an engine room mechanic in the laser room of a starship.

Chapter Eight

As an aftermath of Haldane's slugging match with nineteenth-century literature, he had acquired a taste for tales of lust and violence, which he was satisfying the next morning when a knock came on the door. Turning to the Sermon on the Mount, he left the Bible open and went to answer the knock.

An elderly man, in the neighborhood of eighty, stood in the corridor, a diffident look on his face. "Are you Haldane IV?"

"Yes, sir."

"I'm sorry to disturb you. My name's Gurlick V, M–5, and I was told to come over and talk to you. May I come in?"

"Indeed, sir."

Haldane ushered him in and offered him the chair. He sat on the edge of the bunk while the old man creaked onto the chair, saying, "This is the first time I've drawn jury duty in ten years. By the way, I know your dad. He and I worked on a project about three years ago."

"He died last January," Haldane said.

"Ah, yes. That's too bad. He was a good man." The old man looked off into space in a conspicuous effort to gather his thoughts. "They tell me you were involved with a young lady in another category."

"Yes, sir. She knew Dad, too."

Looking at the old man, Haldane figured there was no point in concealing any theories from Gurlick. At best, Gurlick had only ten years left, and in those ten years he would be concerned mostly with his physical functions.

"The name Gurlick sounds familiar, sir. Did you ever teach at Cal?"

"Yes. I've taught theoretical math."

"Probably I've seen your name in the catalogue."

"Ah, yes. When I learned I was to be on your jury, I called up Dean Brack. He tells me you're a wizard in both theoretical and empirical math. Most I ever did in the other line was to figure out a system for winning at tic-tac-toe.

"Tell me something, son." His voice dropped to a whisper. "Do you ken the Fairweather Effect?"

Haldane's first reaction to the lowered, humble question was almost tears. Here a mathematician, far older than his father had been, was petitioning for information that his father had been too proud to request. He wanted to hug the old man for the bravery in his humility.

It occured to Haldane that the old man could be feeding him a loaded question, one designed to determine his work category. Very well. If this were a classification question, he wanted to be classified as high as possible.

"Yes," he answered.

"What did he mean by 'minus time'?"

"Time in excess of simultaneity."

"Define!" The pedagogue in the old mathematician was alerted, and his voice cracked as he almost shrieked the command.

"The so-called time barrier prevents a speed faster than simultaneity because one solid cannot occupy two places simultaneously. You cannot leave New York and be in San Francisco an hour before you leave, except in earth-relative time, because you would be in San Francisco at the same time you were in New York. You cannot occupy two places at once."

"You make it sound simple."

"My understanding isn't intelligence," Haldane modestly admitted. "You understand Fairweather by a trick of the mind. You have to think in nonhuman concepts. Fairweather explicitly points out the nature of this understanding in his *Jumping the Time Warp*; yet some mathematicians still aren't able to grasp his ideas."

"How could he apply nonhuman concepts to mechanical things, like the Hell ships? Tell me that, young one."

"He didn't," Haldane said. "Starships operate on Newton's statement that every action has a reaction. He contrived a pod of lasers where light converged at a single point to give a push before the beams diverged. The actual principle is the same as that used in primitive jet aircraft."

"Well, I'll be darned. There's no new thing under the sun. I just wish I could live a little bit longer to find out what they'll do next."

"If I had the gift of prophesy. . . ," Haldane started to speak, and precautionary signals flashed in his mind.

He was skirting the periphery of a concept that had come to him, like an aurora borealis, in this deepest winter of his mind, and this particular man was less a juror than a judge.

Strangely, the old man did not look for him to finish the sentence. Instead, Gurlick turned his watery blue eyes toward the window and in a most lovable and absurdly human manner scratched himself. The frail veined hands, fluttering about the dessicated crotch, aroused Haldane's compassion. If this old professor was tricking a student, then Haldane was his own grandmother.

"Ah, yes. I've been having a lot of trouble with my kidneys lately. I don't reckon I'm long for this world, but I just can't help wondering what they'll do next."

He was balanced so precariously on the edge of eternity that Haldane feared for him. Yet, within that skull encompassed by its parchment skin burned still the naïve curiosity of a child or a mathematician.

"I'm a lousy prophet, sir, but maybe they can break the light barrier. You can't be in San Francisco before you leave New York, but then you don't have to be in New York."

"People are always rushing. . . . Son, I was supposed to find out what your feelings were about people, whether you'd rather work with a group or whether you'd rather work alone, but I've got to go. If this trial comes out badly for you, have you got any job in mind you'd like to do?"

"I don't mind working with a small group, and I like to work with laser beams."

"Ah, yes. You're pragmatic. I'll remember that. . . . Well, I don't want to keep you. I'll be getting along."

He got up slowly and stuck out his hand. "Thanks for inviting me in. I've enjoyed talking with you. Could you direct me to the lavatory, son?"

Haldane helped him to the door and showed him the lavatory across the corridor. As he walked hurriedly away, Gurlick called back, "Give my regards to your father, son."

Turning back into his cell, Haldane was saddened by the decline of a mind which apologized for keeping him, forgetting he was a prisoner, and sent regards to a man who had been dead for more than three months.

Haldane's melancholy evaporated with the arrival of his second interviewer.

Father Kelly XXXX had an impossible dynastic number, the result of an internecine battle for status between the Jews and the Irish in the Church. A group of Irishmen in the clergy had arrogated unto themselves numbers reaching back long before the Starvation, basing their numbering system on their known ancestors who were priests. The Jews countered with *their* ancestors reaching back, possibly, to Jesus. Apparently, Father Kelly XXXX had decided to include ancestors who were Druid priests.

Father Kelly's impossible number suited his personality. He was incredible.

Across the board, win, place, and show, Haldane had never seen a more handsome man. His long, black tunic fitted his tall, broad-shouldered body with military precision. His lustruous black hair and brows were balanced by the high gloss of his white collar. His thin, slightly tilted nose looked so sensitive that Haldane expected it to quiver. His lips were thin, his jaw was square with a cleft in the center, and his skin had a pallor that on another might have appeared unwholesome, but on Father Kelly XXXX it was the perfect background for the dark hair and eyes.

His eyes, deep-set and piercing, were so brown the

irises were almost lost. They focused with the power of a hypnotist or a fanatic, and they were at the same time the most unattractive and the most compelling feature of his face.

If it were possible for a man so heavily endowed with rugged beauty to have a strong point, Father Kelly's strong point was his profile. From the side, his features seemed carved by a master sculptor who had lingered for years over the shape of the nose and the line of the lips.

Haldane knew this one. He had appeared often on local television presiding at the burial rites of famous actors. On camera he was handsome. In person, he was overwhelming. He made Haldane regret the size of the cell.

With an engaging smile and the self-conscious worldliness of a man of God, Father Kelly's first remark after introducing himself was, "My son, they tell me you lost your head over a bit of tail."

"Yes, Father."

"It happened to Adam. It happened to you. It could happen to me." He motioned Haldane to be seated on the bed, but he himself walked over to look out the window. There was nothing there but an alley. Flaxon's eyes had not even focused on the view, but Father Kelly looked upward, and he seemed to be drinking in the sunlight.

"Yes, my son, I think it could have happened even to Our Blessed Savior, for he was acquainted with women of whom it might be justly said that chastity was the least of their virtues."

It was an unusual remark from a priest, but it underlined Father Kelly's "regular fellowness" and Haldane was able to relax slightly. If he had a preference in priests, he preferred the regular fellows, even though he had found that their regularity was often strained to the point of irregularity.

"Now that you mention it, Father, I'm sure that Jesus must have been as attractive to females as he was to males."

Suddenly the priest turned and looked directly at Haldane, those eyes pinning the prisoner against the wall. "My son, do you repent your sin?"

Kelly's sudden piety after his freewheeling impiety

94

caught Haldane off guard, and his friendly feelings toward the priest were slashed by the word "sin."

"Father, I regret, surely. . . . But. . . ."

"But what, lad?"

"I hadn't thought of it as a sin. I had only thought of it as a civil offense."

Again, the affable smile came over the priest's face. "No, I wouldn't suppose you would judge it a sin. Not a man alive likes to admit he's sinful."

He looked away, this time toward the door, his chin slightly tilted, and the held gesture flooded Haldane with insight. Father Kelly was a vain man. He had walked to the window to get the best light, and now he was showing his profile.

When he turned again to Haldane, his plastic features had shifted. There was hauteur in his eyes and primness in the lines of his lips. "You can't judge, but I can. Mathematics is your business; morality is mine. I tell you bluntly, my son, carnality is a sin."

"Father," Haldane unconsciously felt his lips grow primly decisive, "I have known carnality in its manifold forms, in the houses sponsored by the state, and my relations with the girl bore the same relation to those experiences as the sacred bears to the profane."

"You misjudge the relationship," the priest said harshly. "The affair was carnal, and, being carnal, it was sinful. We sin when we hurt someone we do not wish to hurt. You have hurt yourself, the girl, and the state. Your sin is threefold.

"You have sinned, my son, and you will spend the rest of your life doing penance. Whether you spend it in prayer or not is up to you. Our Holy Mother does not wish to see you punished. She wishes to forgive you. But there can be no forgiveness if there is no recognition of the sin."

Strange lights flickered in his eyes. Fervor grew in a voice that rose and fell, filling the cell with its vibrations. Then the priest looked away, tilting his profile.

"Father, I'm not being punished by the Church. I'm being punished by the state."

"Ours, my son, is a triune state. The Church is its third leg."

"Then, sir, if I am being punished by the state, the Church is sinning against me."

"My son, I said that to sin is to hurt someone we do not wish to hurt. The state wishes to hurt you."

"Father, you just said Our Holy Mother does not wish to punish me."

"My reference was to Mary, my son."

Kelly's sophistry coupled with his self-adulation triggered antagonisms in Haldane. He remembered Flaxon's warning to project humility, but no image could be projected to this monument of piety because it was so intent on its own projections that all incoming signals were drowned by the signals going out.

Haldane could not resist matching sophistries, so he posed a question in full meekness, with his voice reeking of humility. "Father, Jesus told us to love one another. Does the Church wish to punish me because I have loved another?"

Father Kelly reached in his cassock and brought out a flat case of cigarettes. Walking over, he offered one to Haldane, who refused, partly from fear that he might light the filter end. Father Kelly lit his own and returned to the north light.

He had not answered, but the bent head demonstrated that he was meditating the problem, and the slightly superior smile on his lips told Haldane that he was not meditating the profundity of the question but how best to phrase it to a simpleminded mathematician.

Haldane did a little meditating himself. He didn't like to pass moral judgments on experts in morality. Besides, his interest now was purely clinical; he had a researcher's desire to find how the thought processes of the priest worked. But he was intrigued by the possibility that Father Kelly had received divine grace and had overlooked the package which was lost among the other gifts that God had heaped upon him.

Father Kelly looked up, smoke curling from his nostrils. "My son, when Jesus said, 'Love one another,' he meant precisely that. We must love one another strongly

96

enough to respect each other's social rights. When you attempt to bring unauthorized life upon this overcrowded planet, you are not loving *me*. Jesus said, 'Let us love one another.' He did not say, 'Let us make love to one another.' "

He could not match sophistries with this man. The priest was matchless, on earth or in heaven. Haldane had skirted the edge of disaster by baiting him, for that veering mind, energized by righteousness, might seize on him as an apostate, even an anti-Christ, and his case would be ruined.

He lifted humble gray eyes to the black beads of the priest. "Thank you, Father, for enlightening me."

In a twinkling, the hound of heaven became the shepherd surrogate gazing benignly on his lamb. "Come, my son, let us pray."

They knelt and prayed.

Brief though the ceremony was, it had a tremendous effect on the priest. Father Kelly XXXX had arrived in Haldane's cell as a lissome, smiling, regular fellow; he walked out as a one-man ecclesiastical procession.

Brandt, the sociologist, was Haldane's third interviewer.

"Was that Father Kelly ahead of me?"

"Yes, sir."

"Haldane, observe the wisdom of the state. When it comes to miscegenation, that man's an expert."

"You know him."

"I was once a member of his parish, but I fled with my mate—I hope before it was too late."

Suddenly Brandt's attitude changed to one of serious concern, backed by a candor that was refreshing after Kelly's histrionics. "Haldane, you're in a bad way. It was damned careless to get caught. The state expected great things of you. For a man with your brains. . . . Let it pass.

"There's a lot here I don't understand. How the impregnation occurred is beyond me. Without it, I could have gotten you off with a reprimand. . . . And Cal has one of the best houses in the state.

97

"I checked with Belle, incidentally, She was thunder-struck, angry, and sad. You had that house sewed up. She told me the other students were amateurs compared with you.

"Hell's sleigh bells! How did you ever fall in with a professional, and a poetess at that?"

"She was helping me on a research project."

"Research! What were you researching, the copulatory rhythms of female poets?"

"Nothing as interesting as that. Basically, I was working on an idea that would have eliminated her category completely."

"With her help?"

"She didn't get the social implications. I'd started out to help her write a poem on Fairweather, but when we found out that Fairweather's biography was on the proscribed list, we gave up on him. I persuaded her to help me invent an electronic Shakespeare."

"It's easy to see how you persuaded her. . . Now, I'm in favor of eliminating nonfunctional categories, but weren't you arrogating privileges that didn't belong to you? We in the department decide on which categories to eliminate or create."

"Yes, sir. But you're talking in terms of completed projects. This idea was only in the tentative stage." Haldane slapped his fist against his palm. "Brandt, you may think I have delusions of grandeur, and I would not have presented this idea to you until the program could be demonstrated, but I *know* you would have accepted the idea. Hell, the pressure from the Department of Education would have killed you if you had turned it down. It would have come through channels, but I would have spread the word, unofficially."

"Perhaps we would have," Brandt agreed. "I've got about five categories on my list, and poetry's one of them."

He rubbed the side of his neck speculatively, and Haldane waited while he gathered his thoughts. Suddenly he placed both hands flat on the table and leaned toward Haldane.

"I've got a proposition, Haldane. I'm the foreman of

this jury. Theoretically my job's administrative, but in cold fact I swing a lot of weight. I'm offering you a deal, straight across the table. After tomorrow you'll be a working stiff, so you won't be able to testify against me, so I speak without fear of prejudice. Follow me?"

Haldane nodded.

"I'm prepared to recommend to the judge that you be permitted the highest degree of clemency. That means you choose any job you·wish not associated with professionals. With a project such as yours, it means that you can continue to work on it. As a privileged prol, you'd be given working facilities and raw materials."

"What's the gimmick?" Haldane matched his language with the surprisingly blunt language of the sociologist.

"The gimmick is this: you can continue to work on your project provided you work concurrently on a project of my choice."

Haldane alerted. There had been no change in Brandt's open and easy manner, but his fingers, undulating over the table-top, reflected his inner tension.

Haldane said slowly, "What is the concurrent project?"

"Eliminate the Department of Mathematics."

"That's my department!"

"Correction. That *was* your department."

Fighting to control his facial expression, Haldane asked, "What makes you think I could?"

"Dean Brack told me you were his top theoretical man. If you could do it in literature, mathematics should be easy. We have computers that can solve any mathematical problem we're interested in, but we need a translating machine to convert verbal instructions into mathematical concepts."

Haldane flinched at the idea, but his instincts told him that Brandt was correct. A cybernetic translator could be built. But why had the suggestion come from Brandt? Surely mathematicians had thought of it before.

And nothing had been done about it!

"Hell, I could do it with one hand, but why eliminate the department? It's far removed from yours."

"Greystone's pushing to reopen the space probes. If space were to be opened up, society would become dynam-

99

ic, expanding, exploratory. Social values would lose out to scientific developments. We've got to guard against that possibility."

So Haldane was not alone in his dream of reasserting the spirit of man. Vast forces were joined in conflict in the upper reaches of government, and he was being asked to join the wrong side.

"Suppose I failed?"

"You'd be relegated to general assignments of your own choosing."

"If I succeeded?"

"We would attack again."

"Attack what?"

"The Department of Psychology."

"Brandt," he said, trying to manage a smile, "if you succeeded in eliminating categories wholesale, there wouldn't be anything left to govern, so you'd eliminate yourself."

"I'll worry about that!" Brandt's voice was harsh.

"Suppose I refused?"

"Then you take your chances with the judge—unprejudiced, of course, but still chances."

Brandt was offering him immortality, the immortality of a Marquis de Sade or a Fairweather I.

No doubt such propositions had been offered to thousands of mathematicians in the last two and a half centuries but only one had accepted. Brandt was offering him immortality, or a chance to die in a noble tradition. Unknown to Brandt, there was a third card face down on the table which could eliminate Brandt, but Haldane might be eliminated first. Himself he was willing to risk, but not the Department of Mathematics, not with Greystone in it.

"Run along, Brandt. I'm no Fairweather I. I won't build your pope."

Brandt arose and left. There was no farewell handshake.

At the lunch break, Haldane mulled over the interviews.

After Flaxon's drilling, he felt like an overtrained athlete. He had braced himself for an onslaught of penetrating questions cleverly designed to trap him into revealing atheistic, atavistic, or antisocial attitudes. Instead, he had had a fumbling conversation with a senile old pedagogue, been subjected to the ranting of a religious fanatic, and offered a bribe by a sociologist.

Only in one prediction had Flaxon been wrong. The sociologist had not been verbose; on the contrary, his speech had been very much to the point.

He thought he had held to the image of an eager young student who had inadvertently gone astray, but none of the jurors seemed particularly interested in his image. They had their own problems.

Haldane looked forward to the psychologist, and he was not disappointed.

Glandis VI, his fourth interviewer, belonged to a line stretching back to the very beginning of selective breeding. He was blond, shy, and hardly older than Haldane. He wore the manner of a professional hesitantly—he was deferential.

After shaking hands, Glandis turned the chair around and sat in it backward with his arms folded over the back, his eyes roving over the cell. "A psychologist is supposed to have empathy, and I have plenty for you."

"I need it. This was a rough jolt. . . . Incidentally, you aren't the first psychologist I've dealt with professionally."

"Have you been psychoanalyzed?"

"Back when I was six or seven . . ." Haldane told him the story about the flower pots.

"That explains the microphone. It's worried me more than Helix has. As a matter of fact, I have no trouble at all understanding Helix. She's very nice. One might say, in rhyming slang, she is an outstanding member of the Berkeley Hunt."

Although he was not familiar with rhyming slang, Haldane suspected the compliment was very personal, but he was interested in the psychologist's remark from a legal point of view. Flaxon had said that the girl would not be personally involved in his trial.

"Did you see her?"

"Like a fool, yes. I'm not familiar with jury duty, and I

didn't know I wasn't supposed to talk to her. But she didn't hurt your case. All she wanted to talk about was Sigmund Freud, and all I wanted to do was listen.

"That girl really reads. She's read more Freud than I have. Right now, she tells me, she's getting a lot of consolation out of reading the poetry of that Browning woman. . . . Says it does her good to read about another woman's troubles."

His heart warmed to the message that Helix had gotten to him. All she could hope to say was crystalized in the sonnet, "How Do I Love Thee," and it was her legacy to him.

Haldane even warmed to the unconscious bearer of the message, who was rambling on boyishly. "I tell you, Haldane, you can't sublimate the libido completely. When I was about seventeen I had this strange but strong reaction to a daffy female named Lolopratt. She carried around a Pekingese in her lap and talked baby-talk. I'll never forget that Peke, Flopit she was called. The little bitch bit me.

"Did I kick the dog? Not on your life. I learned baby-talk. Can you imagine a girl like Helix talking baby-talk?"

"Helix is a brilliant female, but I never thought of her as an opposite sex until the day of the funeral."

"Oh, no?" Glandis' remark was a question marked by a skeptical grin. "I would say that you need psychoanalysis."

"Well, I didn't think of her to the point of getting declassified."

"Y'know," Glandis said, "sometimes I think punishment for miscegenous conception is out of line. Take the offspring, I say, rear it, and refuse the parents mating privileges.

"Give the offspring a chance. It's possible the little bastards would make professional material."

"You've got an idea there," Haldane agreed, spontaneously. "Why not just deny the parents their quota of children and see what happens to the child. Mathematically it's almost impossible to breed for a specific personality trait with more than a hundred million variables in any one fertilized ovum."

"Maybe you're right," Glandis said, "but the geneticists have something in their favor. Look at the old Jukeses and Kallikaks, look at the present-day Mobile Blacks. Look at race horses."

"There are traits, outside of physical features," Haldane pointed out, "which might be the result not of genes but of parental environment. Culture's a more important factor. The world's greatest mathematician might be rolling a wheelbarrow right now."

Glandis slapped his leg in agreement. "You've got a point. Environmentalists never had a fair hearing. That Freud's responsibility! If we'd listened to Pavlov. . . .

"You know why the environmentalists never got a chance? Because the robber barons gained control and made genetics a sub-department of Biology, answerable to Sociology. If Psychology had control of breeding, some surprising things might occur."

"We'd better not discuss those things," Haldane warned him, "for they verge on criticism of the state."

"This is a privileged conversation," Glandis said airily, "and to me the state is the Department of Sociology."

"I take it you don't care for sociologists?"

"Oh, I like them all right as individuals. Some of my best friends are sociologists. But as a group they rate low on the Kraft-Stanford scale, only two grades higher than us, and we rate fifth from the bottom."

Haldane grinned at the candor. "If your two categories rate so low on the group intelligence scale, how is it you're one and two in the hierarchy?"

"We're social thinkers. Other categories are like sheep, nibbling at the grass in their own pastures but never lifting their heads to look over the fence. You mathematicians, for instance, are happy little fetuses in the womb of your own problems. You don't take the broad view.

"We psychologists take the broad view, so we're the executive vice-presidents in charge of conditioning. Sociologists are merely administrators. There'll always be a need for the conditioners. When the process is completed, there'll be no need for administrators. The sociologists shall wither away."

Haldane was no longer sure that his favorable first

impression of Glandis was correct. He didn't like the glitter in the young man's eyes.

"You'd be in control, Glandis, but in control of what?"

"A perfectly unified social order."

Since they were discussing a society a thousand years hence, Haldane felt free to rebut Glandis. "Say you achieve this perfect social order wherein the sheep graze under the shepherding eyes of the psychologists. There's only one slight error. Absolute unity means the shepherds are the sheep. There'll be no sociologists *or* psychologists. As a psychologist, your function is to explore the individual, not to erect a social order."

Haldane pounded his palm slowly as he tried to reduce his ideas to a level Glandis could understand. "If unity is the aim of your conditioning, and that aim was established by the sociologists, then you are being tricked. You will wither away into the mass, while the administrators will ever remain above your conditioning."

He could see doubts flicker in the eyes of Glandis, and he pressed on. "Your province is the man, not all men. Your duty is to help the expansion of the individual. In a state where all perfectly conform to each other, there's no need for the Kraft-Stanford Index or the men who created it. There is no scale unless there are differences to measure.

"Glandis, you are destroying yourself at the will of manipulators more skilled than you, the sociologists."

Glandis had listened intently. Now, with a troubled expression, he got up and laid a hand on Haldane's shoulder. "Forgive me for deriding your category. I did it to make you angry, because I knew you'd never speak freely to me in a juror-defendant relationship.

"You see," he took his hand away and walked back a few paces, "I know your intelligence rating is high, and I needed your help."

He turned back to the chair, and when he sat, this time, his hands clenched the back of the chair. "You see, our problem *is* the sociologists.

"Take for instance their practice of diverting men's energies in those houses of prostitution. A brazen use of the pleasure principle, an opiate for the masses. If we could close down those houses, what wonderful aberrations of behavior would occur, what neuroses would flower!

"Think of the guilt feelings that self-stimulation alone would produce. We would have a harvest of case histories. In my five years as a practicing psychologist, Haldane, I've found one lousy case of skin rash diagnosable as psychosomatic. No ulcers. No alcoholics. Only suicides. Lots of them, but never any with individuality. They jump out of windows. Always, they jump!"

Glandis folded his hands across the back of the chair and lowered his head to his hands. He stared glumly at nothing, saying nothing. Haldane felt guilty.

Finally, Glandis aroused himself. "Once I interviewed an old economist, a deviationist on his way to Hell, and he cowered before the overpowering fear that the state was reaching the final synthesis of the ultimate thesis and ultimate antithesis. He was a blithering neurotic, and we had a lovely, lovely interview."

He sighed aloud. "There aren't any nuts anymore."

Glandis clung to the memory of his one neurotic as the tide of his blood pressure swept back to normalcy. Then he looked at his watch.

"I've got to run along, Haldane, but there are a few routine questions I'm supposed to ask. You ready?"

"Ready."

"Which baseball league do you root for in the World Series?"

"Neither."

"Do you have a favorite team?"

"Conceivably the Orioles, or the New York Mets, or the Kansas City Braves."

"Who do you think will win the Cal-Stanford game in December?"

"I couldn't even guess."

"Do you have a favorite sport?"

"Judo."

"Would you rather read a book or go bowling with the boys?"

Haldane idly slapped his fist in his palm. "Now you

105

have me. There are two variables, the book and the boys. It would depend on them."

"Did you love your father more than your mother?"

"Yes."

Glandis raised an eyebrow. "You seem definite there."

"I didn't know my mother. Remember?"

"Ah, yes. . . . Well, that about wraps it up for the Department of Psychology." He stood up and shook Haldane's hand. "I've enjoyed our little bull session, Haldane. You've given me food for thought. . . . By the way, I suppose your lawyer told you that your job assignment depends on the degree of clemency granted. This is off the record, because it's none of my business, but have you thought about what you would like to do?"

"Hell, I don't know, Glandis. I'm pretty shook up, seriously. I feel that for my own peace of mind I should do something difficult, not necessarily pleasant. Maybe I could sign on as a mech with one of the starships."

"Brother, are you sticking your neck out! . . . Well, if you're completely off your rocker, I'll remember what you want when I make my recommendations to the court. . . . Good luck, Haldane. I'll see you tomorrow."

Flaxon listened intently to Haldane's report later in the afternoon, and he was not surprised when Haldane told him of the bribe offer from Brandt.

"They work like that," he said. "There's a lot of rivalry between the departments.

"He offered you a business proposition. He didn't threaten you if you didn't take it. Probably you had a chance to get off the hook, but if you didn't care to take it, that was your decision.

"He could have been testing you to see if you'd sell out your own department. If that's true, your answer was the right one, because loyalty to your department is evidence that your conditioning is bona fide.

"Glandis worries me most. Psychologists are alert to criminal tendencies, and the fact that you established rapport with him means nothing. If he acted hostile, you'd stand mute, and he'd never be able to evaluate your personality. Maybe you talked too much when you mentioned the Hell ships. I don't know.

"Anyway, it's over. If you handled them, I can handle the judge.

"Try to get a good night's rest," Flaxon finished. "I'll see you in the morning at court. I'm working up a humdinger of an opening plea for clemency. If you want to, you can testify in your own defense, but only to rebut points made by the prosecutor. Meanwhile, try to minimize your natural anxiety. You won't be able to do it completely, but I've got a good feeling about this hearing."

Strangely, Haldane did sleep well, long into the early hours of morning, until he was awakened by a memory that floated up from his subconsciousness.

He remembered the name of Gurlick. It had not been listed on a catalogue at the University of California. It had been in the bibliography of a book he had read on Fairweather Mechanics. He was credited with being one of the fifteen men on earth who possessed a full understanding of the Simultaneity Theorem.

The man he had patronized as a senile old pedagogue was a mathematical genius.

Chapter Nine

IT WAS MISTING RAIN WHEN THE CAR TAKING HALDANE to the courtroom wheeled into the traffic pattern circling Civic Square. He saw loiterers huddling like wet chickens on the benches, and he envied all people who had sense enough not to come in from the rain.

From Civic Square the courthouse presented an airy, soaring façade, with its attenuated Doric columns of pink plastimarble. From the alley into which the car was shunted, it resembled a mausoleum with a single narrow slot in the center, the prisoners' entrance.

Flaxon, waiting in the anteroom, fell in beside his client. "In preparing my speech for clemency, I took a leaf from your book and dug into the literature of the primitives. I've got the defense of Leopold and Loeb interlarded with the trial of Warren Hastings and shored up by Lincoln's Johannesburg Address. If you've got the jury, I've got the judge."

Flaxon's enthusiasm was not shared by Haldane, who was still troubled by his delayed recognition of Gurlick. Images could be projected two ways, and if Gurlick was not the bumbling, forgetful person he portrayed, then he was a much more accomplished actor than Haldane.

In the courtroom, most of the spectators wore communicator designations. Henrick was there, and he stuck out a bony hand as Haldane walked down the aisle to wish Haldane luck.

"Friend of yours?"

"Not exactly. More of a wellwisher. He's on the *Observer.*"

"It printed three articles, all favorable. Sob-brother stuff."

"He's trying to soften my fall."

The courtroom sloped to a level area before the bench, above which was carved in the wood panels the slogan, "God Is Justice." From the walls, right and left, projected the slender tubes of television cameras which were used in trials of public interest.

As they entered the courtroom, Haldane's escort, two deputies, dropped behind, and Flaxon steered him to counsel's table before the bench. "The prosecutor," Flaxon said, "is that man at the table to the left who resembles a buzzard. He's Franz III. He might try to blister you a little to offset the *Observer* stories, but it's a cut-and-dried case as far as he's concerned."

"He'll present the evidence: Malcolm's deposition, the tape recording, the medical report, and, probably last for dramatic effect, the damaged microphone.

"I'll enter a plea of guilty to throw the trial into a clemency hearing. Then I'll make my plea, and you can sit back and listen.

"Jurors don't testify in crimes against humanity. They

submit their reports to the prosecution and the judge. The prosecutor can rebut my plea or stand mute. If he rebuts, then you have the privilege of rebutting him, *vive voce*, through me, or in writing. Written rebuttals aren't generally used except in cases involving technical decisions, because their length might adversely influence the judge.

"Malak is judge," Flaxon was saying, "and he's apt to doze. If I can keep him awake, half our battle's won," when Haldane noticed the thin-necked Franz get up and sidle toward them.

Grinning, he walked up to Flaxon. "Counselor, try to keep your clemency plea to less than three minutes. I've got an important meeting I want to attend this afternoon."

"Don't worry, prosecutor," Flaxon assured him. "I'll see that you don't miss the first race."

As the two attorneys engaged in a learned debate over a horse in the third race at Bay Meadows, Brandt entered the jury box. Gurlick was already present, dozing in a corner seat, with Father Kelly beside him. Only Glandis was absent.

As Franz returned to his table, Haldane said, half-peeved, "You lawyers don't seem to take court very seriously."

"Why should we?" Flaxon grinned. "It's not our tails being hung out to dry." Then, noticing the nettled look on his client's face, he added, "Don't worry. We appreciate the gravity. But there's a certain amount of give-and-take in courtroom procedure, and we're begging for a little give right now.

"Ah, here's a wrinkle." Concern broke into Flaxon's voice as Glandis emerged from a door behind the bench, nodding to his fellow jurors.

"What's wrong."

"Psych's been in the judge's chambers. I hope he went in to wake him up."

"Is that bad?"

"Not necessarily, but it's unusual. He could have gone in to get a clarification on a point of law."

"That's understandable," Haldane said. "This is the first time he's ever had jury duty."

"Did he tell you that?"

"Yes."

"He was lying," Flaxon said bluntly. "He's especially assigned to jury duty because he's a specialist on the criminal mentality."

Feeling a cold apprehension, Haldane turned to his lawyer. "Point of honor, department members never lie."

"All truth is relative. A lie told to advance the cause of the state is the truth in the eyes of the state."

"Do they teach you that in law school?"

"Not in those words, but we learn fast. You and I used a similar ploy on the jury."

True, Haldane thought, but there had been integrity in the image he and the lawyer had created. They had highlighted areas of truth and diminished other areas, but nowhere had they perverted the facts. Glandis had lied outright, and Gurlick had lied obliquely.

His train of thought was broken by the entrance of the bailiff, wearing the shoulder patch of a court officer. He entered from the judge's chambers, picked up a gavel, and rapped three times on the bench.

The audience arose.

"Hear ye, hear ye, hear ye, the court will come to order. Ye are here gathered in the fifteenth district court, prefecture of California, Union of North America, World State, to hear pleadings in the case of Haldane IV, M–5, 138270, 3/10/46, versus the people of the Planet Earth. It is charged that he did willfully and without sanction commit miscegenation. Presiding Justice is Malak III. Court is now in session. Remain standing."

Malak emerged from his chambers, black-robed and white-haired, and his eyes, sweeping the courtroom, were alert and commanding. For a moment, they considered Haldane with alert curiosity. Haldane felt that this man would not sleep on the bench.

When he sat down, the spectators sat.

Malak directed the prosecution to present the evidence.

Franz seemed bored as he read aloud the deposition of Malcolm testifying that the student believed an illicit liaison was occurring in his parents' apartment, giving the address, entered it as Exhibit A, admitting it was hearsay but in the light of subsequent findings would stand.

The medical report on Helix was entered as Exhibit B.

Haldane listened with detachment until Exhibit C was introduced, the tape recording of Helix' and his voices that the microphone had picked up and transmitted.

Perhaps it was a deliberate act on Franz's part, or perhaps it was a mechanical flaw, but the playback was slowed to give his and Helix' voices a deliberate tempo which replaced their nervous tension with a tone of calculation. His own voice weighed proposals to thwart foreseen contingencies.

Anger flooding his mind was dispelled by the whisper of Flaxon in relief and disbelief. "You conned Glandis, boy. He isn't even presenting the wrecked microphone as evidence."

Then he heard the judge intoning, "Evidence is admissible. How pleads the defendant?"

Flaxon, rising: "Guilty as charged, your honor."

"Does defense wish to enter a plea for clemency?"

"Defense so wishes, your honor."

"Proceed."

As first pleader, Flaxon walked forward into the arena, partly facing the judge and partly facing the jury. "Your honor, gentlemen of the jury. . . ."

In the beginning his words were halting, groping, as if he were unsure of himself. He told of the first meeting at Point Sur, an accident turned coincident by the introduction of Helix into the Haldane home by the father, honored department member. His voice rose higher, increased in tempo, and Flaxon was a one-man Greek chorus weaving the skeins of the lives of Haldane and Helix together with the inexorability of fate.

As he continued, his voice gained in poise and intensity, and his emphasis subtly shifted to a boy, naïve and innocent, slowly drawn into a maelstrom by the swirls of mortality until, going under, he reached out, and the deed was done. "Premeditated?" Flaxon's voice rolled with the thunder of indignation, then dropped to the whisper of falling rain. "No more premeditated, honored sirs, than the bursting of a morning sunbeam in a dew-drop on the petals of a rose."

Some of the speech was overdone, Haldane felt, but Flaxon was playing to the groundlings, and he was playing well. Random clicks from steno machines began to pick up volume and merged into a subdued murmur.

Flaxon heard the sound, and it propelled him to more sincere heights of rehearsed rhetoric, and he carried his audience with him. Flaxon was doing more to create a favorable impression for Haldane than all the Henricks of the world.

Haldane, mentally apart, admired the lawyer although he would have wished for a deeper, less artistic argument. But there were no more Clarence Darrows on this planet, and so he applauded the first generation Flaxon. Whatever might come of the Flaxon dynasty, its founder was acquitting himself well.

Only one person in the courtroom was unmoved by the argument—Franz. He was reading a document on his table, and not until the sudden applause, quickly rapped into silence by the judge, marked the end of Flaxon's speech did he look up.

Haldane knew applause was out of order, but if the reaction of the spectators reflected the feelings of the judge, he felt that first-degree clemency was assured.

"What says the prosecution?"

Franz stood up. "Your honor, on grounds of evidence in the jurors' report, I move that the charges of miscegenation brought against Haldane IV by the people be dismissed."

Haldane's exhilaration as he turned to Flaxon was squelched by the consternation on the counselor's face as he looked at the prosecutor. "Isn't that good?"

"What says the defense?" Malak asked.

At the moment, defense was occupied. "It can be good, of course. But it's highly unusual, particularly for Franz.

"He's a wily bird. It could be something in the medical report."

112

"But he said the jurors' report," Haldane pointed out.

"True. But Glandis interviewed the girl. He could have added an addenda to the medical report relative to the girl's compulsive libido, which he'd be qualified to do as a psychologist, and the addenda would be in the jurors' report."

"Wake up, defense!" Malak was losing his judicial balance.

Haldane's mind was nettled by the implication in Flaxon's words, and his uneasiness was supplemented by Glandis' remark that Helix was a prime member of the Berkeley Hunt. Had the boy department member been theorizing, or had he spoken from experience?

Flaxon was on his feet. "Your honor, may I ask the indulgence of the court for five minutes while counsel clarifies point of law to defendant?"

"What says the prosecution?" Malak asked.

Flaxon turned to shield his signal from the bench and held up one finger on one hand and four on the other. Haldane quickly deciphered the code to the prosecuting attorney: if he granted the indulgence, Franz saw the first race; if he didn't, Flaxon would stall the hearing into the fourth race.

Franz promptly intoned, "Indulgence agreed to."

Flaxon sat down and began to draw hasty diagrams on his note pad: "Here's the situation, law-wise. If Franz knows the girl is a nymphomaniac, and I don't object, you're home free. The state will drop the charges against you to get at the girl . . ."

"She's no nymphomaniac!"

". . . but if I don't object, and the girl is a police pigeon, you're hung out to dry, because he can slap a deviationism charge against you . . ."

"She's no stool pigeon!"

". . . and since I haven't objected to inadmissable evidence—that jurors' report—it will still not be admissable in the second phase, and we wouldn't have the chance of a lone ember on Hell to prove entrapment. The police would never volunteer to admit conspiracy."

"Helix is not a nymphomaniacal stool pigeon!"

"Agreed! There's the beauty of Franz's maneuver. He knows we know she isn't both—the police would never let her out of the station house.

"But if I object, and she's a nympho, you're swacked! It would be maximum punishment for you, exile to Pluto, because her punishment is geared to yours and she'd be shipped to Pluto on the next rocket transport. You would be innocent, but you'd have to go along because we've already pleaded you guilty."

"I would be innocent?" Haldane was dazed by legal subtleties.

"M'Naughton's Rule—any man able to understand right from wrong, any normal man, that is, has no recourse but intercourse with an aroused white-livered female, lawyer's slang for a nympho."

"But why Pluto? Why doesn't the state send pros?"

"Pros crack up in penal colonies. Their clients are low, bestial, stinking, debased degenerates—which is just fresh meat to the nympho felons."

"That would be no place for a gentle-minded girl of eighteen!"

"Agreed," Flaxon said, "unless she's developed a fondness for low, bestial, stinking, dirty, depraved degenerates, but the girl's not my client."

"Would I get visiting privileges with her if I were a convict on Pluto?"

"For about five minutes a week, but you'd have to wait in a long line. . . . Now, if I don't object and he slaps a deviationism charge against you, our defense would be based on the point of law that perversion is not necessarily deviation. Admittedly you two conspired to pervert the genetic codes to personal ends, but you committed no overt act to interfere with state policies. You two never got out of that apartment, for obvious reasons, so there could be no overt obstructionism."

Haldane was thinking. Helix read a lot. Any girl who read Freud would read law books for light recreation. She could be familiar enough with law to feign nymphomania and get him off the hook because she loved him. He couldn't accept her sacrifice.

"Let's object."

"It's not that easy. . . . They've got you, if there's entrapment. They won't even S.O.S. you, and it'll be Hell for sure. . . . As they say in law school, S.O.L. antecedes S.O.S. . . . I hate to lose a chance on a nympho even if it means letting a stooly off the hook.

"But the bulk of the evidence points to her being a stooly, and if I don't object, I'll never get a chance to look at the book to determine entrapment." Flaxon was genuinely perplexed. "She could be a nympho; that pregnancy of hers came too easily. Characteristic of amorous haste, avidity, hunger for appeasement. Yet, when reading your manuscript, I got the feeling you were being deconditioned by an expert, which would suggest entrapment. Besides, she lied to you, but that doesn't indicate either nymphomania or police connections."

"Are you insinuating that she is a liar?"

"No. I'm defining her legal position. One thousand truths spoken do not make an honest man, but one lie dropped among those truths marks him, henceforth and forever, as a damned liar. You are my client, and I feel that whatever else you may lack, you have at least the honesty of the maladroit. So I can't define you as a liar."

"I don't follow your legal reasoning."

"When I checked your report, I went to the library and looked up Fairweather's *Complete Poetic Works*. The girl was telling the truth about that four-line poem with the long name, but the 'Lament of an Earth-Bound Star Rover' was on the fourth page in the book."

"Maybe it was torn out of her book?"

"She would have known it if she reads as much poetry as you say she does. It's in every anthology in the public library.

"But our indulgence time is running out. It's your choice, Haldane. If you object and she's a nympho, you're dead. If you don't object, and she's a police pigeon, you're dead. . . . Well, what'll she be, nympho or stooly?"

Dazed by the legal complexities and astounded by the computer mind of Flaxon, he said, "A man can't be trusted to make a decision like that about the woman he

115

loves. . . . You're my lawyer, counselor. Flip your own coin!"

"Personally, I'd like a chance to read a jurors' report." Flaxon was rising to his feet. "Object, your honor, on the grounds that the evidence is inadmissible."

"Objection sustained."

"Your honor," Franz said, "will defense withdraw objection if jurors' report is made admissible?"

"How say you, defense?"

"Defense will withdraw."

Haldane, watching, saw a smile light the face of Father Kelly XXXX, who was seated directly behind Franz. Almost as a reflex, the priest tilted his face, and Haldane knew; Father Kelly XXXX was getting ready for the television cameras. That benign glow in his eyes told Haldane that Helix was not a nymphomaniac.

"Move granted. . . . Court will recess for thirty minutes to permit defense counsel to read the jurors' report."

"Something tells me," Flaxon said, "that I have not made an error. You can never go wrong if you lean toward the weight of the evidence. . . . I should have known, anyway, that you would have been able to recognize a nympho."

He got up and went to the judge's chambers as the deputies stepped forward to stand beside Haldane.

It was difficult to believe that she, with all her resources of intelligence and charm, would be an undercover agent for the police. He was sickened by the thought.

But he had to shrive himself of emotions. Experience and logic should have taught him by now that anyone could be anything. Flaxon was a lawyer.

He focused his attention on the sweeping hand of the clock to the right of the bench and watched as it eked out the time with grudgingly granted seconds. Finally, behind him, he heard the rustle of returning spectators, and Franz, Flaxon, and Judge Malak emerged from the chambers. Flaxon moved woodenly to the table as the deputies stepped back. His eyes were glazed. He took his seat beside Haldane as the deputies moved back and Malak motioned the bailiff to the bench.

"She was a pigeon," Haldane said, "and I'm sunk."

Flaxon did not look at Haldane. He was talking to himself. "I'm the pigeon," he said, "and we're sunk. My fifth pleading. . . . Most lawyers never see one. Old Flaxon gets his on the fifth pleading. On *my* fifth . . . on my *fifth* . . . on *MY FIFTH*!"

Haldane shook his shoulder. He was in a state of shock.

His attention was drawn from the lawyer by the bailiff, who was ending his "oyez" with, ". . . to hear pleadings in the case of Haldane IV, M–5, 138270, 3/10/46, versus the World State, the charge being deviationism."

Haldane was no longer charged with a mere crime against humanity; he was charged with a crime against the state.

Red lights flashed on above the television cameras, and Haldane knew from experience what was happening beyond the courtroom. Raucous arguments in friendly family taverns would cease. Conversations and the clatter of silverware against china in public restaurants would stop. Housewives would watch gladly as their television serials were interrupted.

As the crowds had gathered five centuries before at the foot of Tyburn Hill, they would gather now, but they would not be gathering to watch in simple fascination as the hooded hangman opened his trap to innocent death. They would thrill to an enlarging terror prolonged into the sentient agony of a living death.

The bailiff was calling the roll of jurors, and now Haldane knew with certainty that the men who answered to the call were no longer his evaluators but his executioners.

Back when he was mentally competent, Flaxon had assumed that Helix was "right" in saying that that poem had only four lines. As Haldane watched the Third Ice Age of his mind crunch down on him, he knew with intuitive certainty that four lines were all that "Reflections from a Higher Place, Revised" had ever possessed. Helix had composed the others seated across the table from him at Point Sur.

She had planted those lines knowing that she would meet him again and use his doubts to destroy his loyalty

117

to the state. When the police led him away, the triumph and exultation in her eyes had sprung not from an ecstasy of shared martyrdom with her lover, but from delight over the success of her nefarious plot.

As a murderess of loyalties, she had succeeded better than she knew, for his loyalty to her was dead. Perhaps, as Flaxon inferred, she was not a police pigeon, but she had betrayed him, and now she was dead, gone to her death bed, and the cold winds were beginning to howl over the grave where he had buried her.

Helix was gone. His father was dead. And Flaxon was in a state of shock.

He would ride the starships, not as a laser room mech but as cargo on a one-way trip to Hell.

Chapter Ten

As a member of the senior department and as jury foreman, Brandt, the sociologist, was first on the stand.

He had foreseen the direction of the trial, for he had made preparations. Behind him, the bailiff rolled out a tripod on which a large chart was hung. Brandt angled the chart to give the judge and jury a partial view, but it was head-on for one of the television cameras.

"Your honor, I beg the indulgence of the court beforehand for the brevity of my report, which is based purely on a sexo-sociological profile of the defendant elicited from a review of transitory phenomena to project an overview of the defendant in relation to the peer group in which the subject belongs, on a vertical plane in a most cursory manner because this dimension will be, I'm sure, handled adequately by my esteemed colleagues, contrasted to the socioeconomic groupings surrounding his peer group and related to it on a horizontal level, no pun intended, consisting of verifiable, empirical, objective data which lend themselves to hard-core analysis in the sexo-sociological areas, because my departmental duties are pressing; so I must not only apologize for the brevity of my report and for my reliance on your honor's tolerance of subjective analysis of horizontal in-depth factors, but further request to be excused from the continuance of the proceedings after the finalization of my report."

"Permission granted," Judge Malak said. "Continue."

Haldane wasn't positive what permission was being granted, and, thinking himself inattentive, decided to concentrate more closely on what the sociologist was saying.

"In the field of sexo-social behavior, apart from recreational values, the unmated student is practicing a form of status-seeking within peer groups and between peer groups, as was pointed out in the monumental study of the subject by Merk, Baltan, and Fring, to whom I wish to extend my thanks. I have compiled a chart showing the Grossinger Curve for six representative groups, not random samplings, ranging from the theologians, here . . ."— Brandt walked over and pointed to a nubbin on the chart which covered hardly an inch of the approximately 36-inch width of the chart— ". . . to the students of mechanical engineering, here." The M.E.'s drew a whistle from the audience. Their bar covered roughly 34½ inches of the depth.

"Adjacent to, and two inches lower, I mark the students of mathematics." Haldane felt a negative pride in his own department when he saw the bar. His department excelled, but it was only second. If the boys in math had known they were second, they would have tried harder.

"From the two extremes, students of mechanical engineering students of theology, we have established a norm for all students, discounting the summer recess and eliminating statistically such fringe deviations as self-stimulation, mutual participation, and isolated cases of self-enforced celibacy which exists, even in the mechanical engineering and mathematics students with a bias toward theology, as a form of reverse status-seeking. But, your honor, this overview of the field means little in itself except as a prelude to the rather outstanding, or, more precisely, astounding, analysis of the subject in relation to

119

the defendant's peer group, and particularly in relation to the defendant himself. Your honor, in respect to the court, I must confess a certain awe in regards to the sexo-sociological profile, analyzed within the peer group, for the years 1967 and 1968, of the defendant himself. If it pleases the court, may I present for your edification the sexo-sociological profile of Haldane IV!"

With a dramatic flourish, he reached over and ripped the top sheet from the overview; beneath, in the form of a graph, the red line of Haldane IV was impressive when contrasted to the blue of his fellow mathematicians and the bright purple of the mechanical engineers.

"Your honor, I wish to point out to the court that though the index is based solely on the Berkeley House of Recreation statistics, the possibility of social mobility was taken into account by the department and a dossier was prepared of the defendant which included a mobile photograph and a detailed analysis of his techniques which included a *modus operandi,* wearing a wristwatch with a sweep second hand to time the stimulus-reaction period of his co-participants and the use of a peculiar circular movement known on the University of California campus as the "Haldane swizzlestick," characteristics which received positive identification without photographs from areas extending as far north as Seaside, Oregon, and as far south as Pismo Beach."

Pointing to the chart, Brandt continued, "If your honor will note, the chart is divided into three time periods, 1967, 1968, 1969. In the periods of 1967, his freshman year, and 1968, his sophomore year, the defendant *single-handedly* lifted the entire percentile rating for his category by .08. Further note, your honor, that both the purple line of the M.E.'s and the blue line of his peer group—without him—continue through March of this year, but the red line of Haldane IV stops on September 5, 1969, the very date of his accidental meeting with the then-virgin and extracategorical student, Helix, now held in custody, whose condition, pregnant, is attested to by Exhibit B, on file with the clerk. . . ."

"He's hung you by them," Flaxon groaned.

He knew he was hung. Brandt rambled on, wasting

120

subordinate clauses for the better part of half an hour to prove such drives could not possibly be sublimated to the invention of a computer, however complex, but must have been spent in dalliance with Helix.

Then Franz called Gurlick to the stand.

It was slow going for the old man to get to the witness box, and he brought no props, but he made it unassisted. When he spoke, his childish treble seemed to whistle into the microphone, but it carried clearly.

"After I put the boy's mind at ease by asking him about his father, whom I knew slightly in a professional relationship, I started to probe the lad's mind for attitudes.

"Judge, if you'll look on line 83 of page seven in that juror's report, you'll find a remark that boy made, namely, 'I may be a lousy prophet but the next thing they'll break is the light barrier.' "

The man who had sent greetings to a dead man because of a poor memory was quoting page and line number of a juror's report.

"Not one man out of a hundred thousand would have said 'light barrier.' It's just not that generally known what Fairweather was talking about, but this young horse knows. The term used is 'time barrier' because it's called the Simultaneity Theory, but Fairweathian Mechanics holds that time and light are, for theoretical purposes, the same phenomena expressed in different media.

"Now, Judge, I can speak to you without fear of contradiction because my language is not spoken in your world and if you go back to your world and tell them what I have said, they will not understand you, and so they can't come back to me; but I tell you, your honor, this stripling has thought of negative light, and you can't think in nonhuman concepts without nonhuman conceptual ability. This means he's as smart as I am, and I don't like that!

"I'm talking to him now, and he knows what I'm talking about, because he's onto the fact that negative light is another name for negative time, if Fairweather was right and he is.

"That boy out there is a sinner. What's worse, he's a

pragmatic theoretician! He hinted around to me that he wanted to get a berth on a Hell ship. That jack wasn't looking for any job. He wanted a laboratory.

"It's my observation, your honor, that sinners don't repent sins, begging the father's pardon. What they repent's getting caught. Chinese remorse!

"This lad wasn't doing any repenting, either. He was going to do himself a little correcting of the error. He was going to try again. He knows what I mean!"

Full well Haldane knew. That vast and secret concept which had come to him in the quietude of a frozen mind, promising his deliverance, was pinned on the old man's exhibition board.

"Now, when he was talking to Brandt, page 76, line 22, he said, 'I'm no Fairweather, I won't build your pope.'"

"I thought those conversations were privileged," Haldane whispered.

"They were. They weren't monitored. Even now, he can't read them aloud. He's quoting from memory."

The old man was rambling on. "You don't talk about a state hero like that, unless you feel you're his equal. . . ."

"I warned you about Jesus," Flaxon groaned. "I couldn't warn you about every damned thing."

". . . That electronic Shakespeare he was talking about putting together in his spare time would have reproduced a brain more complex than any pope's, and he'd have had to do it in eight years if he was going to jump his fence to get to that filly by foaling time, and it took Fairweather thirty years to build the pope.

"I think he could have done it! Judge, now I've got to be excused, but I say this young jasper's got a mind where practical amorality coupled with potential immortality could get my and your jobs, and I recommend putting that mind in the deep freeze."

As Gurlick hurdle-hobbled from the stand, heading for the wings, Father Kelly swept forward, set his profile for the cameras, and delivered testimony far less damaging than his predecessors'. He quibbled only over Haldane's assertion that God was love.

122

"In this bit of sophistry," the priest said, "the defendant struck at the cornerstone of the Church. Without a concept of God as justice, and the concomitant sternness which the Holy Spirit reveals in administering his order, Freud would be revived, Darwin preached, and Darrow would be nipping at our robes."

He even closed on a note of leniency. He would pray that justice be granted the soul of Haldane IV.

Glandis, the boy department member, strode into the arena as purposefully as a gladiator.

"Your honor, before interviewing the defendant I made extensive preparations to establish empathy. Under the assumption that the subject was possibly atavistic, I read the standard text on the personality abberrations which the ancients called 'being in love,' Booth Tarkington's *Seventeen.*

"Assuming that the object of the subject's libidinal fixation might throw light on the subject's personality, I interviewed the object. She gave me a veiled message for the subject which was, in essence, that he should read for comfort the sonnets of one E. Browning, a poetess who was noted for her excess of sentimentality in an era renown for an excess of sentimentality. When the message was conveyed, the subject's eyes lighted and his whole demeanor expressed happiness.

"With acute insight, I knew that I had established empathy and uncovered atavism.

"Following techniques of ingratiation laid down by the psychology of police interrogation, I expressed the view that the penalty for miscegenation might be unduly harsh since the possibility existed that the products of antisocial births might be socially useful.

"Sensing an ally, the subject demonstrated that the theory of selective eugenics was mathematically unsound and that environmental factors might cause its success.

"I would like to point out to the court that the theory of environmental psychology has been pronounced heretical."

Flaxon responded automatically. "Objection!"

"Sustained," Malak ruled. "Heresy immaterial."

"After initial ingratiation," Glandis continued, "I selected anger-stimuli and aroused subject's ideo-aggressions by deriding his category. His response was to deride my category for failing to develop individual personality, thus subconsciously championing egoism over conditioned reaction or individualism over the greatest good for the greatest number. It is valid to point out to the court that this concept is non-Aristotelian, anti-Pavlovian. It is sheer Freud!

"During this period of the interview, I glimpsed the malfunctions of a social psychopath. In reviewing reports of other jurors, I noted his preoccupation with the personality of our noble hero, Fairweather I.

"His interest in the ideas of Fairweather I were consistent with a youth in his category; but his antipathy toward the state hero indicated a sadomasochistic love-hate relationship.

"This man sought a personal god! He rejected the socially approved worship of Jesus merely because it was socially acceptable. He rejected Fairweather I merely because he was a state hero. This man wanted a nonintegrated, nonvictorious, nonconformist, non-state-approved god."

Listening, Haldane felt a chilled fury howl across the icescape of his mind. No police conspiracy this, but vile entrapment by state officers. He had been baited. Even the most casual side remarks of his jurors had been lures for a trap, and this moist-fleshed, fish-lipped lad, seemingly so innocuous, was a master baiter.

"In the routine National-American League question, his reaction, naturally, was negative. He was indifferent to group sports and equivocal about group recreation, a finding amply supported by the data collected without in-depth analysis by the Department of Sociology. But he was *very* interested in the individualistic, competitive, self-aggrandizing sport of judo.

"Your honor, the full extent of the subject's antisocial orientation came in his answer to the job placement question: he *wanted* a job in the Hell ships!

"Sir, millions have been spent to create in the subject's mind a neuropsychotic Hellophobia, and that horse . . . the subject has balked." Glandis throbbed with incredulous indignation, and his fishface was lifted to the god of mackerels to witness this abomination.

"Then I asked myself, your honor, if the state has failed in this major area of his indoctrination, in how many minor areas must it have failed?

"Here was no mere atavism. I assembled the profile and fed the data into the department's personality analyzer.

"Your honor, out of 153 items indicating a Fairweather Syndrome, the subject scored on 151. A simple majority is enough to carry.

"The time bomb has not exploded, but it is ticking away. There is no psychosis because there has been no overt action, but there," he pointed his finger at Haldane, "sits a fully ripened Fairweather Syndrome. The department of psychology is to be complimented for this discovery."

He turned and faced the judge. "Superficially, the defendant was charming, candid, and persuasive; had it not been for the training given to me by my department, this sociopsychopathic genius would be roaming the solar system unchecked. My initial suspicion was alerted by an idle gesture all others overlooked, the indication of sublimated aggressiveness in his practice of swinging a clenched fist into an open palm.

"May my claim for the department be so entered on the records of the court."

As the judge pronounced, "Clerk, so enter." And as the victorious Glandis walked back to resume his seat beside the remaining jurors, Haldane turned to Flaxon. "A question, Counselor. If Fairweather's such a pariah, why was he permitted to build the pope?"

"The syndrome was not named for the mathematician," Flaxon said. "It was named after his son, Fairweather II."

"Who was Fairweather II?"

"A wild-eyed revolutionary who organized an army of dissident professionals and prols to overthrow the state. You can see what a feat that was! You got no further than one girl and one stupid lawyer before you were caught."

"I never read about it in history books."

"Do you think the state would publish a manual for

revolutionaries? The only people who know about it are those who have to be on guard to detect it, people like lawyers, sociologists, psychologists . . . some lawyers, that is!

"This case ends the Flaxons. You don't defend a Fairweather Syndrome, you report it!" He lowered his head to his hands. "Ninety-nine per cent of the lawyers go their lifetime without even hearing about one, and I get one on my fifth pleading."

One segment of his mind sympathized with the abject man beside him, but curiosity brushed aside his concern not only for Flaxon but for himself as Haldane asked, "What happened to the army?"

"Crushed! Fairweather's father found out and told the police. They were waiting for him when he struck. The uprisers took over Moscow for a week, blew up a few power stations in America, sacked Buenos Aires, but it was all over in three days.

"One good came of it. They analyzed Fairweather's personality before they carted him off to Hell, so the state's been on guard ever since . . . everybody but me, that is."

The voice of the bailiff cut across Haldane's thoughts. "Will the defendant stand?"

Haldane stood.

Judge Malak leaned forward and studied Haldane with curiosity, as if he wanted to impress on his mind the features of one who possessed the dread syndrome.

When he spoke, the judge seemed detached. "In view of the findings of the court, Haldane IV, it is mandatory that judgment be held against you. However, I am suspending sentence pending your appeal until 2 P.M. tomorrow afternoon, remanding you to the custody of the Church, and may God show justice toward your plea."

Haldane sat down as the rustle of departing spectators rose around him, the camera lights flicked off, and the deputies closed in. Turning to the wooden-faced Flaxon, he asked, "What court are we appealing to?"

Flaxon rose, put his folio under his arm, and said, "It isn't us. It's you, though heaven knows it's my last chance

126

too. And you aren't appealing to a court. You're appealing straight to God."

He turned and walked away, not briskly, as Haldane looked sadly on the vanishing back of the first and last of the line of Flaxon.

Franz, he noticed, was already heading through the exit. He'd make the first race at Bay Meadows.

Chapter Eleven

THEY APPROACHED MOUNT WHITNEY FROM THE SOUTH-east after swinging in a wide arc over Bishop and the western edge of the Inyo Mountains, buttonhooking the arc at Death Valley to soar, almost at right angles, into the massif of the Sierras.

In the front seat of the plane, between Father Kelly and a deputy, Haldane watched the wall of granite before them, vegetation stringing its sides where brooks tumbled from the snow fields. Below them, the moraines of the Panamint and the dunes of Death Valley formed a desolate approach to the City of God.

"There it is," the priest whispered in awe.

Haldane shared his feeling. They were gliding low enough and close enough to feel the immensity of the mountain atop which perched the cathedral built to house the machine men called the pope.

Drifting toward the cathedral, like still-winged butterflies converging on a single flower, white pilgrim ships began to float beside them, but there was no alteration in the flight path of the black plane carrying Haldane. Petitioners to escape Hell had priority over pilgrims bringing praise; God's justice was swift.

West of the cathedral was the landing field, shaved from solid granite, on which the ship alighted. It was not much larger than an oversized football field, and it was crowded with pilgrim ships.

Leaving his prisoner to the deputy, Father Kelly jumped from the plane and landed to crouch on his knees, facing the cathedral, his eyes closed, muttering Latin sentences. Haldane and the deputy crawled out as the priest finished his prayer with: "Mea culpa, mea culpa: Haldanus maxima culpas."

The deputy made a hasty sign of the crossbow but remained standing, his eyes on Haldane. Haldane did nothing. He did not consider the cathedral a house of God but a monument to parental guilt feelings.

Father Kelly rose. "Follow me, my son."

Together the trio mounted the long flight of steps. They marched past the waiting line of pilgrims who eyed the black uniform of Haldane with hostility because he was going ahead of them in the line.

They were met at the doorway by a gray-cowled monk of the order of Gray Brothers. Father Kelly was greeted respectfully and conversed with the monk in low whispers. All Haldane could catch of their speech was *Deux ex machina,* but he saw Father Kelly hand the monk a card punched with index holes.

The monk took the card and scampered into the shadows of the building.

Father Kelly turned to Haldane. "Brother Jones has been given your trial transcript which is keyed to your dossier, already on file with the pope. He will have it inserted by the time we reach the altar. Come."

Inside, it was dim and cool, and the air was heavy with oxygen. Haldane, looking upward, could hardly see the ceiling so lofty was the cathedral.

Slowly, setting the tempo of their progress to the stride of Father Kelly, Haldane and the deputy walked down the long nave toward the apse and the high altar which housed the pope.

At the nave side of the transept, the priest halted. "It is mandatory that you make your plea without my intercession. Kneel. Speak directly toward the altar in a normal tone of voice. Give the pope your name and genealogical designation. Ask him to review the findings in your case. Tell him that you seek only justice. Plead any circumstance that you think may alleviate your crime. It is customary to refer to the pope as 'your excellency.'

"And be brief," Father Kelly warned, "for others wait for an audience."

As he moved forward to the kneeling pad, Haldane felt the awe of intense curiosity. No matter what the background of its designer, this computer was the most perfect machine ever devised. It needed no upkeep because it repaired its own defects. It responded to the spoken word in the language of the speaker, and Haldane had heard the rumor, surely apocryphal, that if you spoke to it in pig Latin, it answered in pig Latin.

Its decision was final. It had been known to free murderers and to permit deviationists to walk away from the cathedral with their records cleared.

He went through the ritual prescribed by Father Kelly and finished with his one plea for clemency. "I ask not for justice but for mercy, and this I submit in the name of Our Savior. I loved another with a love that surpassed the understanding of my brothers in Christ."

Suddenly a great voice issued from the altar, speaking with tones hollow and mechanically resonant, yet carrying a great burden of gentleness. "This love was for Helix?"

"Yes, your excellency."

There was a silence underlain by the low purr of dynamos, and in that silence hope exploded in the mind of Haldane, flooding his brain with radiance.

That voice had been too gentle to condemn, too kind to wrest an innocent being from his warm, green mother planet and hurl him onto the frozen wastes of Hell. Haldane leaned forward for the words that would set him free, restore Helix to her profession, and give Flaxon back his dynasty.

Then the words came: "It is the judgment of God that the decision of the court is true and just in every respect."

There was a whirr and a click, irrevocable, ultimate, final. Haldane was so shocked he could not get off his knees and remained on the prayer pad until the deputy, with the priest, came and wrested him forcibly to his feet.

Even the acoustics of the cathedral had changed when the pope delivered his bull, the words rolling through the vast chamber. Dazed, Haldane walked between the priest and the deputy into the bright sunlight and thin air of the mountain top. Once beyond the hypnotic influence of the pope, Haldane felt betrayed, and raw fury surged inside him. He turned on the unsuspecting priest. "If that agglomeration of transitors concocted by a moral idiot is the voice of God, then I deny God and all his works."

Aghast, Father Kelly turned to him, his ordinarily pious eyes burning with anger. "That's blasphemy!"

"Indeed," Haldane agreed, "and what is the Department of the Church going to do about it, sentence me to Hell?"

Haldane's ironic logic struck the priest with its truth, and the exultation of the righteous returned to his uptilted face. "Yes, my son, for you there is no God. You will feel His absence in the hour-long minutes, dragging into month-long hours, oozing into eon-long months of the eternity of Godless Hell, and you will suffer, and suffer, and suffer."

Before noon they were back in San Francisco. After lunch, Haldane was returned to the court, and he was surprised to find the courtroom more crowded than the day before. The red lights glowed above the television cameras, the jury was still present, and an air of expectancy hung over the room.

Only Flaxon was absent. Off on some new assignment, Haldane figured, perhaps mopping the courthouse corridors.

Haldane thought that the passing of sentence would be an anticlimax, now that it was known his appeal had been denied, but he suddenly remembered that the sentencing was the point of the dagger. Here was the moment that unified the world into one folk at one folk festival. This was the swish of the headman's ax, the crack of the breaking neck, the height of the trial. They had come to watch him break under the strain, as he himself had often watched when the trial of a deviationist flashed onto the television screen.

Usually, he remembered, the spectacles began with the fawning, obsequious displays of humility from the defendant, who thanked everyone for a fair trial, often shaking hands with individual jurors, and then there was a rising babble of hysteria as the condemned begged for a mercy which could not be granted. Climax was achieved when the felon fell groveling before the bench, kissing the hem of the judge's robe, whimpering, moaning, or falling into a dead faint. Such was the standard form, and it was usually adhered to; it was not considered good form and was not satisfying to the public when felons fainted prematurely.

These things were bread and circuses for the mob and the most effective object lesson the executive departments of the state had hit upon to communicate to the people the horrors awaiting the deviationist.

Suddenly he remembered Fairweather II. Certainly the mind that in secret and alone had almost toppled the Weird Sisters had not cowered before this ordeal, and he had the same personality traits as Fairweather II. Pride of tradition ignited the powder of his anger, and a resolution exploded in Haldane's mind.

He would treat the mob to a different exhibition.

Again the bailiff droned the audience to its feet, the judge entered, and there was the theatrical solemnity of Father Kelly intoning the decision of the pope.

Malak said, "Will the prisoner arise?"

Haldane arose.

"If the prisoner wishes, he may speak to the bar before sentence is passed." Malak's fatherly tone throbbed with eagerness.

Now was the moment for fawning overtures to the jury. Now was the time for him to bow in obeisance and rise babbling for mercy. Speaking in a level voice into a microphone, he began:

"I was born to the honored profession of mathematics, fourth in the line of Haldane. If all had gone as planned, I would have solved problems assigned me, would have mated a suitable female, and would have died in honor precisely as my father died, and his father, and his father."

He paused. That was trite enough and contrite enough.

"Then I met a female whose forfended place was forbidden, but for me she possessed a beauty beyond my telling. As I walked with her in an old world grown suddenly young, I wove her charms into a sorcerer's spell, and under that spell I saw visions and learned much wisdom, I found the Holy Grail and touched the philosopher's stone.

"Mark me, now. In my innocence, that spell was of my own weaving, and, in my ignorance, I was the sole instrument of my doom.

"She lifted me to that high plane of self-awareness and self-oblivion once called by some 'satori' and by others 'romantic love.'

"If I sipped from that chalice hemlock and thought it elixir, I put the cup to my own lips. If the song I heard from the throat of my beloved was the song of Circe, then I would turn again to hear that song, for it was piercingly sweet.

"Let it be known to the court that I do not deny this girl.

"So, I was led to a realization of selfhood, and it was my awareness of myself as an individual, not my love for the girl, which has brought me to the threshold of Hell and branded me a votary of Fairweather II. Since I can speak with unique authority, let it be known that I deny this earth and its gods, but that I do not deny Fairweather II.

"In his wisdom and in his gentleness, Fairweather II, the last saint on earth, adjured men to guard their uniqueness, to preserve some hidden portions of their selves, against the moldings of those who would come to us with persuasive smiles and irreproachable logic in the name of religion, mental hygiene, social duty, come with their flags, their Bibles, their money credits, to steal our immortal . . ."

"That's enough, felon!" Malak leaned over the bench and shouted to the cameramen behind the wall slits, "Turn off those cameras!"

"Hear him out!" a voice yelled from the audience, and boos and catcalls were beginning when Haldane hurled his last cry of defiance before the red lights switched off: "Down with Soc and Psych! Wreck the pope!"

A phalanx of deputies moved from a side chamber to herd the crowd toward the doors. Haldane was surrounded by uniforms. "Get him out of here," someone said.

All the strength and defiance which had driven Haldane left him, and he allowed himself to be pulled and shoved into a barred antechamber. A deputy said, "The chief says hold him here until we get the armored car."

"For Christ's sake, that's high level thinking for you," one complained. "If we move now, we'll get to the big A before a mob has time to form. If we wait around twenty minutes, he'll be lynched."

A deputy turned to Haldane, "I've got to hand it to you, fellow. If you're trying to beat a Hell rap by getting yourself killed, you're pulling a smart trick. Trouble is, you might take some good men with you."

Yet they waited, and when they took him from the chamber to the prisoners' ramp, four cars were drawn up, rifles jutting from ports in their bulletproof windows. It was the first time in his life that Haldane had seen a show of force by the police.

Slowly the procession moved out of the alley. On the civic circle they were met by a heavily armored car with laser guns on the turret, and the procession turned left on Market Street. They drove slowly to allow the sirens to clear the way, and it seemed to Haldane that the spectators were being drawn from the buildings by the sound of sirens to stand woodenly on the sidewalks and watch the procession move along.

Left at the Embarcadero they turned, and always there were people, standing, looking, making no overt show of antagonism toward him. It was as if they were persons in a trance.

As they neared the long, guarded bridge to Alcatraz, Haldane noticed one gesture from the crowd. Before they turned onto the bridge, a woman lifted her hand and waved to him in a gesture of farewell.

Her farewell galvanized his mind.

The deputies had thought he was in danger from the mob, but their thought had been a conditioned reflex. Was it possible that it was the deputies in danger from the mob, not he?

The more he thought of the solitary woman, the more convinced he became that the gathering of the people had been no threat to him. The woman had waved because that was all she knew how to do. In olden times, they might have thrown stones at the deputies or set up barricades to stop the cars, but such reactions had been trained out of them. A crowd could not rally to the barricades if the crowd did not know where the barricades were.

As he was processed into the prison, as his gray guards were changed to blue guards and he walked interminable corridors, he clung to the hope, as a talisman against despair, that the final, forlorn wave of the woman had been a symbol assuring him that the vision of a free people which had driven Fairweather II to Hell had not been a vision in vain.

In the next days, he needed a talisman against despair, for despair beat against his mind as the waves of an ocean, and he succumbed. In a dark midnight of the mind, he lay on a bunk for days, weeks, he did not know, aware only that he was fed intravenously.

In the final, bitter days before his departure, he heard a sound like the whisper of a sibyl come keening into his consciousness with prophecy and promise, arousing him.

He was in a large, high-ceilinged room, surrounded by a balcony where guards patroled. On the floor of the room were individual cells walled and ceilinged by bars that permitted the guards to look down on the occupants. Haldane was in a cell by himself.

Across a corridor twelve feet wide was a large cell housing several prisoners, prols he assumed. He would have ignored them except for the singing which drifted through the vastness of the prison like the keening for a dead soul.

It was a prol song accompanied by a guitar.

The despair which had almost destroyed him acted as a shock treatment, and the brain that listened to the crude singing was as receptive and as uncritical as a child awak-

ened by bird song. The words of the song gave it a hope
beyond beauty.

Let the rains come,
Let the winds blow,
Let the snow fall,
Come the frost.

But there always
Comes fair weather,
There will always
Be fair weather.

In fair weather,
I'm the boss.

Before the song ended, Haldane was on his feet, looking across the corridor at the tank. He saw a huge black
man lounging on a bunk and cuddling a guitar in hands
that dwarfed the instrument.

"Black man," he yelled, "do you know what you're
singing? Do you know who Fairweather was?"

"White man, you mean what fair weather is."

"I mean who Fairweather was!"

"Listen to the thinker. He wants to know from me who
Fairweather was."

From another tank, a voice shouted, "Why does a
thinker have to ask a prol?"

"Fair weather is sunlight, white man."

There was again laughter, scornful, derisive, as if the
laughers shared a knowledge so obvious that even to ask
about it was ridiculous to the point of humor.

They were a motley aggregation, ranging in size from a
pale dwarf to the black giant, who must have stood seven
feet. Some were marked with the yellow of Venus and
some fish-pale from the mines of Pluto. If he had seen
them chained together on the streets of San Francisco, he
would have dismissed them as the scum of the interplanetary working force, but now they were part of his own
habitat and he looked on them as individuals.

"You can tell me about Fairweather," he called, "because I'm a felon sentenced to Hell."

"Man, you got it rough," the black answered him. "Us in this tank's just got to smell a little cyanide gas."

They dismissed him, and he sensed the logic in their dismissal. Why share a cherished secret, if there was a secret, with a doomed man; and if the man was not doomed, then he was a spy.

That night, as the glow from the sleeping lamps blanketed the prison in a blue luminescence, he lay on his bunk staring upward when a paper glider sailed into his cell and landed beside him. He took it, smoothed it out, and moved it over into the light of his sleeping lamp.

We think he was a man like J. Christ or A. Linkun
or I. W. Wobbly. Some clame to no more. My muther
told me he was a good man. TARE THIS UP.

He had established contact, but his mind was troubled.

He tore the paper into shreds, and leaning close to the night lamp so the men in the cell across the corridor could see, he chewed the shreds and swallowed them.

It was obvious to him now that the fair weather song was a song about sunlight. How could it be otherwise when these men, in their illiteracy, had placed Fairweather on the same plane as I. W. Wobbly, who was not a person at all but the initials of an ancient labor union of winetasters. He could not blame the men, but illiterates could neither tap nor preserve their history in writing.

Thinking thus, Haldane made his peace with the world, and his peace was a disavowal. Helix was gone, his father was dead, the professionals were sheep, and the prols were insensate brutes.

God was a computing machine.

He thought that he had ceased to feel, until three days before they came to take him away. And, then, he felt with the keenest poignancy his life had ever known.

"Hey, thinker!"

It was the black, yelling across the corridor, standing near the bars with his guitar draped around his neck by a dirty thong.

136

"Got a new song, thinker. Felon just brought it in from the outside. You want to hear it?"

There was insolence about the Negro. His broad smile, verging on the nonsubservient, aroused Haldane's old professional standards. "When you speak to me, pork-chopper, wipe that watermelon-eating grin off your face!"

"You can't insult me, thinker. I'm a Mobile Black. I been worked over by all them ologists. . . . You gonna hear it, whether you want to or not."

The man was right. During the Starvation, when Negro flesh was considered a delicacy, the Mobile Blacks had escaped extinction by the insularity of their little island off the coast of Alabama. Afterward, anthropologists had kept the race pure, and the Mobile Blacks had been the subject of endless and derogatory monographs by social scientists.

He strummed a few bars and sang:

> There was a man who loved a frail.
> He knocked her up, got throwed in jail.
> The judge he says, "Deny this woman."
> Man says "No, 'cause I'm a human."
>
> Hold up your head, poor Haldane.
> Hold up your head, don't cry.
> Hold up your head, poor Haldane.
> Poor boy, you'll never die.

Before the song was over, Haldane was on his feet, clinging to the bars of the cell.

He had undersold the brutes. Their songs were their history. In one crude stanza, the balladeer had revealed his trial, and in another he had used it to keep hope alive in the minds of men.

The fair weather song was the Fairweather Song.

Three days later they came and dressed him in a gray shroud and led him down the long corridors to the loading ramp where a black car waited to carry him to the launching pad of the Hell ship.

He walked impassively, but his head was held high, and the prisoners crowded close to the bars lining the corridor.

As the crowds had stood along Market Street, they stood and watched woodenly as he was led away, but their lips were moving, almost invisibly, and their voices joined in the final chorus of the words a felon had composed to the tune of an old song which Helix had sang to him once, on a long ago day of sunlight, under the name of "Tom Dooley."

It was easy to hold up his head. The second task came harder.

Chapter Twelve

OFFICIALLY, HALDANE IV WAS A CORPSE.

He was unconscious when the Gray Brothers carried him aboard the *Styx* on a litter. In the food or water he had taken, he had been given a drug to slow the life processes of his body.

So he did not see the line of cowled figures carrying their burdens up the long ramp and chanting liturgies for the dead. He did not hear the ports clang shut or the beginning whine of the rockets. He felt neither the initially slow ascension nor the final whiplash of motion as the great ship tore itself from the pull of the earth, and he did not feel the slight jolt as the rockets were dropped and the laser jets took over, booting the ship with a soundless clang into the iron grooves of space.

Silent, bodiless, immune from the hurtling detritus of space, they moved into a realm where all light, save the light inside the ship, vanished as sound vanishes to ears above Mach 1. They were light, riding a wave of simultaneity that would have sent them hurtling through the core of the sun unscathed.

For three earth months, Haldane slept, and every minute on the ship's clocks reversed a day on earth.

He was awakened by a hand on his shoulder, and he looked up at the coarse-browed, heavy features of a spaceman whose unsmiling face was illuminated by a battle lamp attached to the bulkhead.

"Wake up, corpse. Wriggle your arms and legs, like a beetle on its back. . . . That's right . . . . Got to give you a little pill, a little oxygen booster."

He had been unstrapped from a bunk in a cell, and all he could see in the pale light, besides the face of the spaceman, was a ladder leading upward through the metal overhead.

He went through the motions suggested and felt his muscles respond with a strength and resilience that surprised him.

"Enough," the man said. "You can sit up."

"How long we been away?"

"About three months, our time. Here, take this."

Haldane accepted the proferred tube of water and pill, remembering there were only two starships. There was a fifty-fifty chance that this man had been on the ship taking Fairweather to Hell.

"Tell me," Haldane asked. "Do you remember a corpse called Fairweather who rode these ships?"

"Everybody on board knew him. Back then, we didn't put them to sleep. They rode awake, all the way. He and the other corpses messed with the crew.

"Lord bless me, I never could figure out why they kicked that man off the earth. He was the most gentle person I ever met. If a fly had landed on his plate, he wouldn't have brushed it off. Like as not, he'd have just said, 'Let it eat. It's hungry too.' But his wasn't a weak gentleness. He was strong."

"What did he look like?"

"Tall, skinny, auburn-haired. He didn't look like much but when he got to talking, people listened. But I'm not saying he talked a lot. He didn't. We liked him as much for his silence, I reckon, as for his talk."

The spaceman paused for a moment. "Funny thing, you know. You ask me about a man, and I'll say, 'Old Joe's a good old boy. He hits the bottle a little hard and shoots off at the mouth, but he'll give you his last dollar.' That kind of answer pretty well tells you about old Joe, but you can't do that with Fairweather."

"Try for me, will you?" Haldane pleaded. "It's important."

It was important. Haldane felt suddenly as a worshiper of Jesus might feel on meeting an apostle, and he was burning with an eagerness for the unrecorded details.

"I'll try, but you'll be going back to sleep pretty soon."

"Did he laugh?" Haldane offered a hook for the man to hang his memory on.

"He smiled a lot, but I never heard him laugh. It wasn't his smile, though. It was those silences and the way he talked when he did talk. He would think about what he was going to say before he said it, so that when he said something, it seemed significant.

"Not that he lectured us, mind you. God knows he could have. He seemed to know more about the history of earth than any man I ever talked to, but he wasn't stuck-up about it.

"I guess he was sad. Sometimes there'd come a look in his eyes that made you want to walk over and pat him on the head, but he never complained.

"He wasn't prissy, either. Sometimes he'd say dirty things that managed not to be dirty at all when you thought about what he'd said. Once I remember him telling me, 'Sam, in that aborted crotch of yours are seeds of a better generation than you'll be getting.'

"That sounds dirty, but looking at the younger generation, I think I see what he meant.

"I remember once when I had the watch on the navigator's bridge, he came in and talked to me. He asked about the instruments, how you read them, and whether I liked being a spaceman or not. I told him anybody would enjoy being a hero, and then he said something I've always remembered, and he said it in sort of an offhand way, like he wasn't even thinking about it. 'It won't be roses, roses all the way. I fear you're seeing the last of the roses.'

"You know, he was right! We get three days on earth after each trip, and for most of us it's two days too many. It doesn't make a man feel good to go into a bar and have the fellow on the next stool move down three or four places.

"But you want to hear about Fairweather.

"He had a way of listening. You'd sit and talk with him, and he'd fix you with those young-old eyes of his, and next thing you'd be telling him everything ever happened to you. He'd make an engine room mech seem as important as the captain.

"Reserved, I reckon you'd call him, but he had a lot in reserve, understanding, sympathy, maybe you'd call it love.

"It was like—" The spaceman was groping for words, and Haldane wanted to yell to him to hurry because the fog was drifting in, and his voice was fading. Haldane hung on to wakefulness long enough to hear, "—having Jesus riding the forecastle."

When Haldane awakened the second time, there was a different voice in his ears, shouting down through the hatchway, "Rise and shine, corpse. Rise and shine. Shake a leg. Up the ladder, and stand by the passageway."

Slowly, fighting the receding waves of sleep, Haldane sat up. Someone had loosened his belt, and he felt the pull of centrifugal force holding him to the bunk.

With the light in his eyes from above and the voice urging him on, he crawled out of the bunk and scrambled up the ladder.

Tall, long-armed, a spaceman bent down and helped him up the final stages of the ladder. Blinking, he stood in the passageway, feeling his body bent forward.

Holding him by an arm to steady him, the spaceman reached behind him to a locker and pulled out a parka and a pair of fleece-lined boots. "Put this gear on and secure the hood of the parka. We're back in space, and we're circling a thousand kilometers above Hell. You'll be going down in a few minutes. You're in section eight and your letter is K. See that light down there marked 'eight'?"

"Yes."

"When your section's called, walk down the passage behind the corpse marked 'J.' The letter's stitched on its back. Go down the hatch and strap yourself into the seat marked 'K.' After that, your instructions will come from the ground."

He left Haldane and went down the passageway to awaken other sleepers.

Haldane stood for minutes as the cobwebs left his brain and the energy returned to his body. The long sleep seemed to have affected him no more than an afternooon's nap. Swiftly, as a hiker adjusts himself to the psychic load of a newly dropped pack, the balance organs of his body adjusted to the cant created by the centrifugal force, and he was able to don the heavy-weather gear while standing.

"Now, hear this," the intercom crackled. "Now, hear this! Section eight, fall in."

He faced right, seeing the J on the back of the corpse ahead of him. Slowly, guided by a spaceman, the column wended forward, each member staggering as his legs adjusted to a walk, and descended the hatch marked 'eight' into the interlocked hatch of an airplane appended to the hull. Haldane was the last corpse in the line.

It was a narrow opening that led into a nested ship which would be cast off from the mother ship when the lugs were released. Clambering down into the dimly lighted plane, he found the seat marked K and strapped himself in.

Above him, he heard the pneumatic wheeze of a closing port, and the hatch above him was sealed. Through the metal surrounding him he could hear a voice over the intercom of the mother ship saying, "Stand by to cast off eight."

Then, far away and remote, he heard for the last time a voice of earth, calling "Cast off eight."

There was a metallic click as the lugs disengaged, a wheeze as the exit hatch opened, a light forward movement as the plane was hurled along its short, grooved track, into the darkness a thousand kilometers above Hell. Then came weightlessness. They were falling through cold and darkness, drawn from airless space by the pull of the giant planet beneath them.

There was no apparent motion. Haldane craned his neck and looked out through the small port beside him.

For the first time, he gazed on the home of the earth's rejected, the frozen planet, and he was amazed.

In the pale light of a distant sun, a part of the planet was visible. On one side was the shadow of the night, but on the lighted side he could see the snow-covered surface, but it was not all white. There was a black expanse rippled by clouds which he knew was an ocean. The sight which drew him up short was the sight of sinuous lines drawn over portions of the snow field that were not concealed by clouds.

There was no denying the contour of those lines joined by lines. As the falling craft came closer to the planet, his wonderment became knowledge. The lines represented a river system drawn over the white surface of a continent.

The rivers of Hell were not frozen.

There was a gentle bump as the plane hit the atmosphere and leveled off under the guidance of an automatic pilot. There was a perceptible heating of the interior. He felt the drag cups of the plane strike the mass of air, throwing him slightly forward, and slowly the sensation of gravity filled the cabin.

They were volplaning down, boring into the night of the planet. The sun was lost, but a huge moon hung motionless in the sky.

Suddenly, well into the shadow of Hell's night, the plane banked into a circle, focusing on a small point of light far below which flickered intermittently between drifting clouds. Slowly, in ever decreasing circles, they volplaned down, gliding through a thick overcast to emerge into moonless blackness.

The vehicle straightened its flight path and nosed down. He felt the crunch of runners striking the snow, heard their high, metallic squeal. The craft skittered and yawed, then straightened in a long, diminishing skid toward the point of light. Then it slowed to a stop.

Haldane IV had arrived on Hell.

As soon as the swish of the plane's runners ceased, there was a clambering on the fuselage and a door beside

143

him opened to let a gust of cold air enter from a night so dark the blackness seemed to enter the cabin.

"All out, on the double!" The command came from the darkness, and Haldane, closest to the door, unstrapped himself and stepped out onto the door ramp and onto a crust of snow impacted as solid as stone.

Beside him was a squat figure, dimly illuminated from the glow from the plane's cabin, and the voice that came from it seemed heavy with unvoiced curses. "Step lively! As soon as the door's closed, the plane returns to the ship."

Dim figures tumbled through the doorway with alacrity. Apparently satisfied with the speed with which the exiles were moving, the man stepped back, waiting, and Haldane asked, "Are your nights always this dark?"

Though asked in disarming sociability, Haldane's question was loaded. He felt he could determine by the man's answer if he were a convict guard or another exile whose harshness was the natural tone of Hell's inhabitants.

"No. Tonight we have clouds over the moon, and there's a blackout on the field."

His voice was absurdly gentle, the voice of a teacher speaking to a backward child.

Undaunted, Haldane asked, "Why do you have a blackout?"

"We don't want that ship up there to know we've got lights. But we have, and lots besides. Some night, when that bastard's orbiting up there, it's going to meet a chunk of metal coming from the opposite direction."

There was no doubt about this man's status; he was an exile.

To the shadowy figures gathering around him, he said, "Step back and let your eyes get adjusted as I close the door. Then follow me. If you get detached from the group, make for that point of light. If you get lost on this planet, you're dead."

Keeping his eyes on the figure of their guide, the group trudged off through the snow.

It took them ten minutes to reach the landing field shack.

Inside, it was warm and well lighted, and a coffee urn

144

in a corner filled the room with aroma. There were rough wooden tables and wooden benches, more wooden furniture than Haldane had ever seen before.

Their guide threw back his parka and said over his shoulder, "There are coffee cups and cream and sugar by the urn. Help yourself. Your guides into town will be here in about fifteen minutes."

He turned and went into an area separated from the main room by a wooden railing. In the corner of the area was a radio transmitter, and Haldane, ignoring the coffee, watched him as he sat down at the transmitter and spoke into a microphone. "Joe, this is Charlie. The Marston Moor group is in. Three couples and two singles."

"Five of them, on their way."

"Are the lights on?"

"Three more minutes."

"See you, Joe."

After Charlie signed off, Haldane asked, "What's the pressure and oxygen content of this atmosphere?"

"Twenty p.s.i. at sea level and twenty-eight per cent."

"Where does the coffee come from?"

"From coffee beans, for Christ's sake!"

"Two lumps of sugar and a dash of cream, coming up!"

He turned at her voice to see Helix coming toward him with a mug of coffee in her hand, moving with the willowy grace of old and the poise of a hostess at a Cap and Gown tea. He was mildly surprised to see her, more surprised to see her slender figure, and amazed at her smile which glowed with the self-satisfied pleasure of a woman who has kept a surprise party secret from her mate. There was nothing guilty about that smile.

He accepted the coffee and sipped it. It was delicious, aromatic, winey but at the same time fullbodied. He tried another sip and the taste was not illusory. "I had an idea I might run across you here. Flaxon figured you were prime material for this planet."

"Who's Flaxon?"

"He's a man who mops floors at the San Francisco

145

courthouse. But you should be . . ." He finished his sentence with a hand movement.

"As big as a grounded blimp." She finished the sentence for him. "At my request, the doctor suspended my animation three days after I was arrested. I was positive the state would send you here."

Something was radically wrong with his estimate of the situation, so wrong he decided to practice discretion. Something told him that recreation facilities on this planet might be less than adequate, and he did not wish to jeopardize any potential source of supply.

"How were you sure you were coming?"

"Because I read history books. A papal bull issued in 1858, the famous 'guilt by association' decree, exiled all mates of deviationists to Hell as co-deviationists."

"Suppose they had not discovered I was a deviationist and merely S.O.S.ed me?"

"I knew they would spot you," she said. "I recognized your Fairweather Syndrome from the very first day we met. Anyway, I had the doctor revive me on the day you were sentenced. I couldn't miss the show.

"But I wasn't about to wait eight years just to take a lottery chance on a genetic chart. I took direct action."

"So that accounts for your security lapse. But what makes you think I'd mate with a girl who is not a virgin?"

"You already have, by papal decree."

"The pope's not infallible on Hell, and you can't claim legality on a lawless planet."

She shook her head sadly. "Logic was never your strong point, mate. I checked the stats before I made my move, and males outnumber females five to three on Hell. Before I spoke to you, I was casing that gray-haired gentleman looking out the window. He looks very lonely and in need of a woman's sympathy."

He sipped his coffee, and looked over the other two females. One was a dumpy blond going to fat and the other was too boney. Both were well over twenty-eight.

Someday he would outfigure Helix, the day after he had found the formula for squaring the circle. The only stupid

146

act on her record was laughing at him for being in love with her. Who had followed whom to Hell?

"I'll take you," he said. "Now take this stupid cup so I can overcome my scruples about kissing a woman on the mouth."

He worked up to her lips beginning with her neck on a rising tide of giggles and joy in an unseemly public demonstration which drew consternation from the haggard-faced men and possessive smiles from the anxiety-ridden women exiles.

"So, you're mine," he whispered. "How does it feel to be married to a man who never reads *all* of a small book of poetry?"

Her giggle, this time, sprang from nontactile causes.

"I tricked you by deriding Milton. I knew, with your syndrome, you'd be so involved with him you'd never get back to Fairweather. . . . Psychology for the negative child. . . . But I was proud of you, Haldane, and the girls in my block cheered when you didn't break. . . . When you rose to defend my . . . least favorite poet, and me, after all I had done, I broke down and wept."

Tears of pride and relief were beginning to form in her eyes, and to keep the demonstration from becoming even more unseemly, he said, "I wonder if civilities are such on this planet that we might introduce ourselves to the other exiles."

"Let's try," she said.

"You won't make a play for the gray-haired man or that dark-haired, fairly young man?"

"You're the only criminal I'll ever mate with," she said.

They had furnished enough diversion to let the watching group relax, with the exception of the old man, who still stood, cupping his eyes from the glare within, and peered out the window.

Their introductions were welcomed. The others seemed pathetically anxious to introduce themselves and to explain the crimes which had brought them to Hell.

Harlon V and his mate, Marta, had been sociologists found guilty of altering the files on workers up for liquidation hearings. Harlon estimated that he and Marta had saved nearly fifty prols from the cyanide chamber.

Hugo II was a Berlin musician whose long and frowsy hair stuck out at all angles. In a thick German accent, he explained brusquely that he had tried to form a group to stop the playing of machine-composed music at state festivals. The fourth man whom he had approached, a musician in his own orchestra, had been a member of the secret police.

His wife, Eva, was far more loquacious. "They came for us at midnight, and they knew all about Hugo. In three days Hugo was tried and convicted. In five days we were on our way.

"Our German *polizei,* ah, they are efficient devils. But my Hugo is efficient, too. All of Bach, in microfilm, is glued into his toupee. So, we have all come, Hugo, Bach, and I, to Hell. Is it not a charming name for so snowy a place?"

Hyman V was an accountant whose forebears had been Pharisees before the Hegemony of Judea. He had been apprehended reading the Torah while wearing a yarmulke. In Haldane's estimation, the yarmulke was as senseless as the impregnation of a female.

Suddenly Haldane's retroactive mind clicked, and he recalled, "I spotted the Fairweather Syndrome the first day."

She had spotted a behavior pattern a lawyer and three trained investigators had missed! How? And how did she even know the Fairweather Syndrome existed?

He had some more explanations coming from Helix.

Hall II, the man by the window, introduced himself last, speaking in an easy, uncowed manner that pleased Haldane.

"I was a teacher, a naturalist, and the state didn't care for my methods, but that's behind me. . . . Listen, I've been looking out the window, and I'm sure I can see trees. Trees mean chlorophyl, and chlorophyl means sunlight. That sun we saw couldn't furnish enough energy for dandelions."

"True," Haldane agreed, "and the rivers aren't frozen."

"The light doesn't come from the sun," Hall swung to Haldane, "unless. . . ." His brows puckered.

"Unless the planet swings in an ellipse!" Haldane said.

"Exactly, son. Perhelion, summer. Aphelion, winter."

Suddenly a look of confusion spread over Hall's face. "But why hasn't earth caught on to what's happening?"

"Maybe somebody back there likes us," Haldane said. "Unless the spacemen have an agreement with Hell. . . . But no. Our boy Charlie. . . . yes! Maybe the captain's afraid to report. . . ."

"Oh, no." Hall objected. "Spacemen are pit bulls. They don't know fear. . . . More likely the schedules. . . . Yes, that would be a possible. . . ."

"Of course it's possible. They never deviate. But the schedules weren't set on Hell. . . ."

Their train of thought was broken by Charlie, who walked over and distributed cards, saying, "Fill these out."

So, Haldane thought, they were even to be categorized, classified, and assigned slots on Hell. He was growing resentful until he glanced down at the card. All that the slip requested was his name, profession, and the reason for his exile. He filled it out, scrawling across the bottom, "The Fairweather Syndrome."

As he finished, he heard a tinkle coming from the outside, drawing closer. He turned to Helix. "That sounds like sleigh bells."

The guide collected the cards, stacked them in a pile on the edge of the table, and went outside to turn on flood lights. Through the opened door, Haldane could see a line of sleighs approaching across the tarmac, drawn by horses that resembled shaggy-haired Clydesides. Then the guide closed the door.

When the door opened again, five men entered, wearing parkas and fur boots. They walked over and picked up the cards off the table, throwing back their parkas. One of the men turned and said, "Haldane and Helix!"

"Here," Haldane said.

The man walked over. He was sixty, with steel-gray hair and thin, strong features. There was friendliness and

149

intelligence in his eyes, and the hand he extended to Haldane was cordial. "I'm Francis Hargood. I'm detailed to take you into town, get you located, and begin your orientation program. This, I take it, is your wife, Helix."

Haldane had never heard the term "wife," but Helix said, "I am, but he hasn't quite adjusted himself to the idea yet."

Hargood's hand to Helix was very cordial. "Then drop him, by all means. It would be criminal to restrict yourself to an audience of one. . . . Haldane, accept your marriage. A happy marriage gives you a good base for operations, and nothing attracts the female as much as a wedding band. Acts as a challenge. . . . Take the first sleigh by the door."

He stood aside as Haldane followed Helix through the doorway. Outside, he said to Haldane, "To my knowledge, which is very skimpy, you're the first mathematician we've had with the Fairweather Syndrome. You'll be welcomed to Hell."

Haldane helped Helix into the sleigh as Hargood went around and solicitously tucked the lap robe under her. Then he got in on her side and slapped the rump of the horse.

"Was the horse imported?" Haldane asked.

"No, home-grown. The flora and fauna of Hell are much like those of earth's temperate zones."

With a toss of its head and vapor wreathing from its nostrils, the horse moved forward, the runners on the sleigh squeaking over the crusted snow, harness bells jingling, heading toward an avenue of lights in the distance that had not been lighted when the plane landed.

The lights illuminated a broad highway cut through what appeared to be a pine forest. When they entered the avenue, the horse broke into a trot. With the crisp air splitting on his cheeks and Helix' hand in his under the lap robe, he felt a beginning joy that almost overrode his apprehensions.

True, the man at the field had been sullen, and the horse-drawn sleigh was a primitive mode of travel, but

Hargood was friendly, and there must be a technology of sorts on the planet since there was electricity and radio.

There was another act on the part of Hargood which had not gone unnoticed by Haldane.

Back in the shack, when Hargood had finished reading the card Haldane had filled out, he had casually torn it up and thrown it into the wastebasket.

"I'm taking you into town and putting you up at the inn with the others," Hargood explained, "but after you've bought clothes and gotten somewhat acclimated, you'll be boarded out until your own home is built.

"By the way," he added, "you two are fortunate. Your presence has been requested at the home of a university man who lives on the college campus. Most arrivals are assigned by lot."

"How did he know we were coming?" Haldane asked.

"He didn't know you by name. He merely asked for the youngest theoretical mathematician on the H drop. He's a very distinguished old gentleman, but quite active. I think he has in the neighborhood of a hundred offspring, so don't leave him alone too long with Helix."

Hargood stroked his chin, "What confuses me is that he was able to figure I'd even have a theoretical mathematician on the H drop or the A or B drop, for that matter. . . . You're the first theoretical mathematician I've ever seen."

Chapter Thirteen

"OUR TOWN IS MARSTON MEADOWS ON THE MOUTH OF the Redstone River; population, forty-five thousand; biggest industry, the university. Since the nearest population center is a copper-mining town two hundred miles upriver, you can see that we haven't made a dent in the planet. But we follow the old Biblical maxim, 'Be fruitful and multiply.' Since we have long winters and no television, the population growth is coming nicely.

"It's an interesting town, mostly because of the university crowd. Some real cuties out there. Head of Economics, otherwise rational, preaches that someday earth and Hell will reunite in the final synthesis of the thesis and antithesis.

"We have some beautiful beaches around here, and I'll prophesy, right now, Helix, that when you walk out on them in a bathing suit, there's going to be a riot."

"Do the natives call the planet Hell?" Haldane broke in.

"Yes, out of deference to Fairweather I. Anyway, Hell means light in German."

"Do you defer to the man who exiled his son here?"

"Our Fairweather II was rash in his youth, so his father sent him here to save his hide. Then he invented the pope to keep his son in high-level bridge partners. . . . Do you swim, Helix?"

"It's one of my favorite sports."

"You'll enjoy Marston Meadows, and Marston Meadows will enjoy you. Most Hell-born women are low-slung with broad bottoms. In a way, they tend to resemble wasps. They're not unattractive; they simply have varying degrees of attraction, and you'll be in the upper two per cent."

"You mean the pope is a trick on the executive departments?"

"Yes. . . . We have some very attractive women's shops in Marston Meadows. They dress more provocatively here."

"I'm sure I'll love sleek gowns and glitter. I can hardly. . . ."

"I cursed the pope!"

"We all did." Hargood turned to Helix. "The fact that you two were mated by the pope doesn't necessarily mean that you're restricted to each other. . . ."

"The planet moves in an ellipse around the sun, doesn't it?" Haldane broke in.

"Yes, so we have four months of winter, three of spring and fall, and two of summer, each half year. . . . Our

152

summers never get tedious, and our winters can be very interesting."

"What is your specialty?" Haldane asked.

Hargood laughed. "Calling a man a specialist on this planet is almost as bad as calling him a son of a bitch."

"What's that?"

Helix laughed. "It's an old expression. It means your mother was a dog."

Haldane fingered the expression in his mind. It was pungent, and he could see where it might react unfavorably on a man who had cultivated an undue affection for his mother.

"Actually," Hargood continued, "I was a gynecologist on earth. . . ."

"I thought you had more than a passing interest in such matters," Haldane broke in.

"Here, I've branched out. I'm a cellist in the town orchestra, on the board of aldermen, and teach in the university.

"Very few men are specialists on this planet. I have eight children by my wife, and seven by the wives of other men, so I'm not even a specialist as a father. Rather unusual by earth standards"—he paused reflectively—"but we do have long winters."

"What does your wife think of this?" Helix asked.

"She has twelve children."

"Why haven't the spacemen reported to earth that this is not a planet of ice?"

"When routine calculations were made by the probes, the exploring crew landed in the dead of winter and figured the planet had only minimal habitability. Fairweather I rechecked the calculations, discovered the error, and set up the schedules of the prison ships so that they always arrive in winter."

They passed the first dwelling, a two-storied structure faintly visible in the light of road lamps. It was made of logs, and its pointed roof mantled with snow, the glow of light in its windows, seemed poignantly cheerful to Haldane.

After the horse clumped over a wooden bridge spanning a wide creek, there were more houses, and the pungency of woodsmoke in the air was exhilarating.

Helix pressed his hand. "It could be eighteenth-century England."

They passed a church made of stone; lamps glowing in its vestibule illuminated scrollwork above the portal which read, "God Is Love."

Haldane called Hargood's attention to the sign. "So you worship a God of love, not of justice."

"Emphatically," Hargood said, "although we may use a rather loose definition of the word. . . . Incidentally, if you were mated by the pope, there must have been a reason. If you need a gynecologist. . . ."

"We'll talk about that later," Haldane broke in.

"You don't seem to be very far advanced."

"I was in suspended animation, voluntarily, waiting for my lover to be shipped out." She looked over at Haldane. "Incidentally, young man, you have a lot of explaining to do."

"About what?" he asked in genuine wonderment, thinking there were quite a few unexplained details that she had to clear up.

"This is not the time or the place. But the place is close and the time is near."

What caprice guided this girl he would never know. On earth he had once been bothered by the fear that he would never be able to plumb her infinite variety, and now the old uncertainties were returning. But of one thing he was absolutely certain with hackle-raising intuition: if the task of understanding her was beyond him, the good Doctor Hargood would be glad to give it a try.

Hargood was looking at her with eyes too openly admiring to be lecherous, giving her some fatherly medical advice. "Of course, at this stage of your pregnancy, your activities won't be too hampered. You can have an uninhibited honeymoon."

"What's a honeymoon?" Haldane asked.

"It's the period when the newly mated couples get to know each other. It's an old earth custom we've revived on Hell."

"I thought we'd already had our honeymoon," Helix

said, "but I've discovered differently. . . . Look, the shops are still open!"

"We're coming into the downtown area. I apologize for our lack of skyscrapers, but we don't need them."

Few of the buildings were more than three stories high. They were close together with brightly lighted show windows on the ground level, and there were a few heavily bundled pedestrians abroad, apparently shopping. Haldane's eyes registered the panorama of lights, decorations and the abundance of goods in show windows, but his mind played almost lovingly over the purposelessness of the people who ambled along the sidewalks. There was none of the precise, straightline walking one met on the streets of San Francisco.

Hargood reined the horse down a narrow street that dead-ended in a courtyard before a two-story building which Haldane assumed, from its many lighted windows, was an inn. Here, the overhanging buildings and courtyard at the end of the lane were suddenly illuminated when a rift in the clouds let the moonlight through, and the glow on the snow gave a medieval quality to the scene.

"Looks like it's clearing up," Hargood said, driving the sleigh in a broad arc to bring it before the inn door.

A boy of about fourteen came running out of the inn to catch the reins that Hargood threw to him. "Hi, Doc," the boy said.

"Hello, Tommy. If you get a chance, will you curry my horse? I'd certainly appreciate it."

"Doc, I scraped that damned brute down to the skeleton this morning."

"All right, Tommy," Hargood said patiently. "Don't curry the horse."

As the boy led the horse across the courtyard to the stable and they walked toward the door of the inn, Haldane asked, "Is it customary for a hostler to deny the request of a professional?"

"That hostler's name is Tommy Fairweather. And there aren't any professionals, as a class."

"I imagine his grandfather would turn over in his grave if he knew a Fairweather was working in a stable."

155

"If he did, it would surprise a lot of people over at the university, because they don't know he's dead. . . . Now, one last ritual, folks. Turn around!"

They had reached the lobby of the hotel, which was empty, and Hargood's command was still a command. Haldane stopped, and did an about-face.

He felt Hargood's hand rip the initial from his parka, the classification initial he had forgotten. Hargood was saying, "There goes your last earthly classification. There are no dynastic numbers on Hell. We use Christian names, old style. Helix is now Helix Haldane. You need a first name."

"Don Juan," Helix suggested.

Haldane was not thinking about names. He turned. "Are you telling me that Fairweather II is still alive?"

"Certainly. He's only a hundred and eighty."

"How long do you live on this planet?"

"As long as you wish. There are methods of retarding cell destruction. They're known on earth, but they can't be indulged. Here, the prolongation of life is almost mandatory."

Hargood was helping Helix take off her parka. Haldane slipped out of his and handed it to the doctor, who took it to a cloakroom behind the desk of the absent room clerk. "It's almost fourteen o'clock, so Hilda, the barmaid, will be doubling as the room clerk."

Through an open doorway, Haldane could see a large dining room; across it, logs were burning in a fireplace. He turned to Helix. "Did you hear that? Fairweather's still alive."

"Oh, no. He's dead. . . . Isn't that a lovely fire?"

She seemed hypnotized by the distant flames, a dream lost in a beautiful reverie.

"Hargood says he's alive!"

"That's Fairweather II."

"That's who I mean, Helix! He's the brush they smeared me with."

She seemed to snap out of her trance. "Of course, dear. But we were researching Fairweather I. I thought you were speaking of Fairweather I."

Hargood returned and guided them into the dining

156

room. To the right of the entrance was a bar and to the left was a stairway leading to a balcony which lined one side of the room. The gloom of the huge room was lighted by individual table lamps, and across was a cleared area with a hardwood floor adjacent to the fireplace and a second bar not being used.

Hargood steered them to the bar. "Hilda," Hargood said, "meet Don and Helix Haldane, newly arrived newlyweds. Give them the bridal suite."

"Welcome to Hell," the woman said, turning to a board behind her and grabbing a key. She was a tall, lanky woman with cadaverous cheeks. Her hips were in a line with her waist, and the expression in her eyes when they fell on Haldane was one of carnivorous hunger. Though her breasts flapped like dewlaps and the twin plaits of her hair were streaked with grey, her hungry eyes created a weird eroticism in Haldane. He knew that if Helix had not been there, he would have remained at the bar.

Hilda tossed the key before him in a manner casual but without insolence. "It's room 204, straight up the stairs."

She turned to Hargood. "Real nice piece of man you brought this time, Doc. Young one, too."

She turned to Helix. "Most of the exiles we get here are in their forties, at least. Your man looks like a lot of action. He's not as big as the average Heller, but he's pretty tall for an earthman. And those arms look strong. If you get tired of him tonight, throw him down to me."

"Funny thing"—her voice dropped an octave as she leaned over to Helix to talk woman-talk—"I get some of my best action from the small, shy men. You never can tell from just looking at them."

Turning again to the trio in general, she said, "What will it be, folks? Drinks are on the house."

"Beer for us all," Hargood said. "And she isn't being generous. For exiles, everything's on the house."

"Why take the wind out of my sails? I wanted them to think I was a philanthropist."

"I ordered beer," Hargood explained, "because I wanted you to taste it. Everything tastes better here."

Hargood went in to a discussion of taste on the planet,

attributing the flavor to the quality of the soil. As his attention was directed almost exclusively to Helix, Haldane's eyes roamed the bar.

Near them sat a slender, dark-haired man, almost raptly sipping a drink as he cast an unbroken series of polite glances at Helix in the bar mirror. Farther down the bar was a giant wearing seaman's boots and a sailor's hat. His mouth was open, and his red beard bristled with a static electricity which Haldane assumed was generated by desire. Haldane's assumption came from a glance at the man's eyes—the most expressive eyes he had ever seen. At the same time they were undressing Helix, they were concocting thirty-six variations—Haldane counted them—on a single theme.

Haldane turned brusquely to Hargood. "Let's go to a table."

"Just a minute." He leaned over the bar and called down to the genteel ogler. "Halapoff, how about fixing up a dinner for eight?"

"Sure, Doc," the black-haired man answered. "When will they be here?"

"Right behind us."

They took their glasses and walked across the room toward a table. There were more than a dozen couples in the dining room, and although the men were accompanied by women, there were low whistles of approval as Helix walked across the floor.

Haldane felt a flash of anger which focused on Helix. She was conscious of the raw undertones to the sound, and that beautiful, free-swinging stride of hers slowed to a mincing step and her face flushed. She was strutting.

His own beloved and pregnant bride enjoyed being whistled at!

Haldane's rising anger was halted abruptly.

As they passed a table, he noticed a red-haired woman whose high cheekbones and erect carriage gave a regal touch to her undeniable beauty, which was accented by a full eight inches of cleavage above her low-cut gown. Her physical beauty was awe-inspiring, her cleavage an act of nature, but the attraction that emanated from her threw up such powerful fields of force that Haldane's stride swerved in her direction.

From a casual conversation with her table partner, the woman looked up, saw Haldane's glance, flashed him a radiant, appreciative smile, and whistled.

Helix caught the contretemps and flashed the woman a look that collapsed her force field and restored Haldane's compass bearings. She reached back, grabbed Haldane's arm, and practically shoved him toward the table. "You liked that!" she hissed.

"You were getting a few thrills yourself."

Hargood selected a table near the fireplace.

Haldane asked what the open space with the polished floor was used for.

"Mostly for dancing. Unfortunately, not always. We've revived social dancing as a recreation because it is stimulating."

Haldane exploded. "Do these people *need* stimulation?"

Hargood laughed. "It wouldn't seem so to a citizen of earth. Hell is literally hell for some earthmen, but very few females from earth are ever unhappy here. All of them are loved and appreciated, especially appreciated. There's not a female without attraction. Some simply have more attraction."

He glanced at Helix.

Haldane sat brooding in his beer. He wasn't a prude, but he certainly didn't care to ride shotgun on his wife whenever she went to the grocery store. He intended to move fast on this planet, and he didn't wish to divert any energies guarding his rear, or his wife's.

"What sort of technology do you have on this planet?"

"Sufficient for our needs, and we have tremendous natural resources."

"Could you build a starship?"

"That's a little out of my line. But I'm sure we could. We siphon the best minds from earth. Why do you ask?"

"I've got an idea for a starship which can exceed simultaneity . . . go faster than now. Have you got a pencil?"

"Are you planning on going back to earth?" Helix asked.

"Not to the one we left."

He took the pencil Hargood offered and began to sketch a design on the tablecloth. "Here's a laser propulsion system. Light emitted from this source, here, streams forward to converge, here, allowing the stream of light to reinforce itself, here. As you can readily see, you're exceeding the speed of light, as we know the speed of light, but the convergence principle, as you probably know, is limited by the focal length to the orifice from the lasers."

"Don, I'm a gynecologist."

"Now, this symbol represents simultaneity, a perfect function of the converging lines. In practice, that function is never reached. For instance, it took us, in actual time, six months to make the four million light years to Cygnus, which figures out at about .987643, considering S as 1."

"But I'm a gynecologist!"

"I had this idea for a series of curved mirrors, arranged thus, in a circle, which would reinforce the original beam from the laser, emitting pulsations, which would reinforce the reinforced speed. A chain reaction. . . . Follow me?"

"No."

"Well, I think the idea's valid, and certain remarks made at my trial reinforced my opinion."

"Don, you've lost me. Mathematics is over my head."

"Forgive me, doctor. I must remember that your interests lie in the other direction. . . . But you can tell me this: what form of government do you have here?"

"We call it a 'democracy,' which is Greek, and it's Greek to me. I don't have a very abstract mind. If I can't touch it, I can't appreciate it. But we elect a president every six years, and he appoints advisers."

"What gets him elected?"

"Wong Lee got in by promising to reduce the police force. Too many people were getting arrested for disturbing the peace. . . . Helix, in planning your home on this planet, you'll have to remember to allow for the construction of extra bedrooms. . . ."

160

Haldane was thinking apart from Hargood and Helix as the two chatted.

If promises were the key to political power on this planet, he would have to find out what appealed to these people. He thought of setting up houses of recreation and installing professional recreational workers, but he immediately rejected the idea. Such sterile entertainment would not appeal to a population that wanted to fertilize and be fertilized.

"But doctor," Helix was saying, "my most pressing problem is clothes. I didn't bring a thing with me."

"We'll visit the clothing shops tomorrow."

"I'll need lingerie and pajamas tonight."

"On your wedding night?"

He might offer state awards for bearing offspring. It was an idea, but the problem there would be to prove the parenthood of the male.

Other exiles had arrived with their guides, had been treated at the bar, and were taking their tables. Apprehension was gone from their faces. On the way to their table, Harlon V and Marta stopped by at their table to exchange first impressions.

Marta had gotten a subdued form of the treatment that Helix had received on her walk across the room, and her air of dignified refinement had been replaced by vivacity and pleasure. Harlon's air of dignified refinement had been replaced by one of hurt dignity. Harlon, Haldane figured, might not be able to stand the competition.

Halapoff, once started, moved fast. Some happy Ukrainian hiding in his ancestry must have directed his preparation of the shishkabob, and he glowed when Helix complimented him on the meal. "He's an even better accordion player," Hargood said, when any further remarks were shattered by a burst of sound.

Beginning on a low rumble and rising to a high-pitched quaver, the sound rose and fell in a prolonged series of whoops. Haldane turned and saw the giant red-bearded man from the bar strutting to the center of the dance floor, his head tilted toward the ceiling, the burls of his fist pounding a tattoo on the barrel of his chest.

"My name's Whitewater Jones. I'm half horse and half alligator. I can walk barefoot on a barbed-wire fence and strike sparks with my feet. I'm a third generation Heller, and the day I was born I clawed out a bobcat's eyes and chewed off its tail. I'm as fast as greased lightning and as strong as a mammoth bear. I've whipped every man and loved every woman between Marston Meadows and Point of Portage. I shoot nothing but live bullets."

Beneath the roar from the dance floor, Haldane asked Hargood, "What's the matter with him?"

"Alas," Hargood answered, "as a nation of individuals, our people go to extremes. This man is a bully, and right now he's going through a fertility ritual.

"He runs the riverboat between here and Point of Portage and only gets to town about three days out of the month. This is his way of working off steam by getting into a fight and getting himself a female."

"Don't you have policemen?"

"We only have nine in the whole town. If they tried to lock him up, they'd be hurt, and they'd have to let him out in a couple of days because he's the only pilot on the river."

It was difficult to talk beneath the roar, and the man's claims were interesting. Haldane listened as he boasted that he had carried his steamboat across a sandbar on his back. Hargood tapped his shoulder. "Don, you'll get two weeks on the house as a honeymoon gift from the pope— and by the way, it's traditional for the groom to carry the bride across the threshold."

Haldane tried to listen, but Whitewater Jones was demanding his attention.

"Halapoff, break out your accordion and play us a tune before I hit you so hard your freckles rattle. None of these earth fillies knows how to dance, and Whitewater Jones is giving them lessons. Get moving!"

Halapoff sprinted across the room to the bar, where Hilda handed him an accordion. It was the most amazing demonstration of persuasion by threat of force Haldane had ever seen. Halapoff was actually frightened.

Hargood made no attempt to discipline the man when

he went swaggering around the arc of the tables, leering at all the women and sizing up, particularly, the women from earth.

"Whitewater Jones wants to dance, and when White-water Jones dances, he fondles. Any female who hasn't been fondled by Whitewater Jones has the biggest thrill of her life coming up."

His swaggering, salacious progress was incongruous against the background of Ukrainian folk music into which Halapoff's frightened fingers were putting tremolos unscorable.

He neared the Hargood table, spotted Helix, and roared, "Doc, are you holding that little chestnut filly back? Let her out of the gate!"

"You've been drinking too much," Hargood said.

"You hinting I can't hold my liquor? I can lift a barrel of hooch and drink it dry without spilling a drop, eat a medic to settle my stomach, and pick my teeth with an earthman's arm."

He stopped and put a massive arm around Helix' shoulder. His roar dropped to a thunderous coo as he said, "Ma'am, I know you earth women don't know how to dance, but waltzing's easy. I'd appreciate it if you'd let me give you your first lesson. . . ."

Haldane rose quietly behind the love-smitten sailor and walked onto the dance floor as he heard Jones say, "I'm just an old country-boy sailor, and I don't get into town much. I'd love to give you your first one. . . ." He raised his voice and bellowed to Halapoff, "Play a waltz!"

In the silence, Haldane called, "Come, dance with me, you son of a bitch!"

In one of those flashes of inspiration he had never been able to analyze, it had struck Haldane that the red-bearded giant might be a mother-lover.

"What did you call me, son?"

From the hurt and disbelief in Jones's question, he felt he might have hit pay dirt. As the sailor had requested, Haldane repeated the phrase and stressed the last word.

This was not mere pay dirt. He had hit the mother lode of mother-lovers. The incredible speed which galvanized the giant, drunken bulk as it charged across the floor at Haldane marked Whitewater Jones as the most affectionate son since Oedipus Rex.

Chapter Fourteen

SEEMINGLY AS SLENDER AND AS INEFFECTUAL AS A GAzelle before a charging rhino, Haldane awaited the charge as Halapoff's accordion broke into a syncopated version of the "Valse Macabre."

When the hurtling Jones passed the spot where Haldane had stood, Haldane tripped him and he skidded the full width of the waxed floor. His head struck the row of empty stools along the service bar and scattered them in a manner so reminiscent of a ball striking bowling pins that someone in the dining room shouted, "Strike!"

There was a scattering of polite applause from the spectators.

Whitewater rose to his feet, felt a cut on his lip, and looked at the blood on his hands. The sight of his own blood must have driven him berserk. Yet, despite the added impetus, Haldane scored only three tables, plus occupants, on his toss into the dining area.

Applause, however, continued in volume.

More important, he had maneuvered Jones into position. On the third charge, he grabbed an extended arm, levered the sailor over his shoulder, and sent him flying through the air to land on his hocks, bounce once, and skid, feet first, into the fireplace, and the roaring flames.

Screams of pain from the fireplace brought prolonged applause from the dining area and the strains of "Waltz Me Around Again, Willy" from the accordion.

Apparently Jones had rudimentary educability. Using his head instead of his scorched feet, he hobbled slowly toward Haldane, making no sudden movement that could be used against him. He advanced on the earthman, his arms extended as pincers, and slowly they encircled Haldane.

He had put his head into the maw of the lion. An audible intake of breath from the audience testified to his mistake and to the fact that he had gained audience sympathy.

Gently, the arms drew Haldane toward the great chest as the massive legs spread apart to give a solid base for the crushing action. But Haldane was not crushed in the slightest.

He lifted his kneecap with explosive force.

With a yowl that exceeded the fireplace whoop by several decibels, Jones dropped Haldane and clutched for his offended area. Haldane delivered a karate blow to the base of the neck. Jones shook the floor as he fell into a fetal ball, clutching two spots, bleeding, and whimpering, "Calf rope. . . . Calf rope."

Haldane had never heard of a calf rope.

He circled the fallen hulk, which had, fortunately, fallen on its right side, leaving the chin open for a kick from a right-footed kicker. He carefully sighted his toe with the point of the chin, and drew back a pace to deliver the *coup de grâce* as Halapoff played "Auld Lang Syne." *Ole's* were issuing from the crowd.

"Stop it, Haldane!"

It was the imperious command of a professional. Years of discipline froze Haldane.

Hargood strode into the arena bloodied by the drippings from Jones's mouth, "When he yells 'calf rope,' that means he's beaten."

"I'm sorry, sir." Haldane apologized. "I'm not familiar with the customs of the country."

"Stand up, Jones. I want to look at that mouth."

Slowly, first to one knee, Jones struggled to his feet and obediently opened his mouth.

"You may lose a tooth, and you've cracked a lip. Go to your room and sleep it off. I'll see you at ten o'clock in the morning."

Shaking his head and mumbling, the half-horse half-alligator stumbled toward a rear door marked with an exit sign.

"Something tells me you're going to adjust well to Hell, Haldane." Hargood took his arm and steered him back to the table.

Haldane was shaking slightly, but not from his exercise, which had been minor.

That jury on earth had been correct in their evaluation of him. Beneath the thin shell of civilization, he was a brute rampant, and tonight the egg had cracked. He felt as if he had staggered from some desert of restraint to plunge into the cool, clear waters of violence. He had intended to kill Jones, and he would have enjoyed doing it.

Before they were seated, Helix said icily, "Did you have to do that?"

"I'm always irritable right after I wake up."

"That poor man only wanted to dance with me. I admit he was rough and crude, but he talked with a kind of poetry."

"Only wanted to dance with you!" Haldane stared at her incredulously. "Are you *that* naïve? If you're *that* taken with his poetry, I'll go drag the bum back, and you can spend my wedding night with him."

"Yes, you will adjust well to Hell," Hargood said, with sad certainty.

"You're very aggressive, aren't you?" Helix was chiding him, but there was an admiration in her eyes which revealed an animalism to match his own. She was the one who had adjusted to Hell. She had adjusted so rapidly that it was as if she were a native of the planet.

"Doctor Hargood, I know you're tired and want to get home to your wife and twelve children, eight by you, so Helix and I will excuse ourselves and retire."

"I don't know if I should go up there with you or not," she said. "You're so physical."

"As the good doctor has pointed out, there's an old custom in which the groom carries the bride across the threshold. I'd like to remind you that there's an older custom in which the groom drags his bride to his cave by her hair."

"I come, master," she said, rising.

Again, that unpredictable inspiration struck.

"I'll carry you," he said, "to make sure."

He threw her, squealing and squirming in feigned anger and true delight, over his shoulder and carried her across the dining room and up the stairs, while the enchanted audience arose and gave him a standing ovation. At the top of the stairs, he turned, waved to the crowd, and patted her protruding rump.

The audience stamped, cheered, and whistled.

He shoved open the door and carried his sizzling bride into a room where a fireplace with a roaring log fire cast lights over a lavish fourposter bed, canopied and curtained. "You crude beast," she hissed, "I felt you do that! I'll never be able to hold my head up on Hell again."

"It was nothing personal," he assured her, pulling aside the curtains to toss her on the bed. "I was keynoting a political campaign, my opening gun in a run for the presidency. . . . It doesn't matter on this planet whether your head is up or down. Three-fifths of the population never look that high. . . . These brutes have a primitive energy which I intend to control, and with a unifying command whipping them into conformity, they can produce the technology my idea will need."

She lay back, tilted on her elbows, and looked up at him in amazement. "Conformity! You fought it on earth. . . . The pope was right! You would have wrecked earth if I hadn't got you off the planet."

"Listen, Helix," he sat down on the bed, intensity etched in every line of his face. "Here's where the end justifies the means. I would be able to free the earth from the stranglehold of the sociologists.

"That chain reaction of light, triggered by a laser source, would mean speeds of infinite acceleration. You see, it's like a pinwheel of light generating within itself such a tremendous force that the propelling orifice need be no larger around than this."

"Quit making lewd gestures!"

"And the thrust delivered through that orifice would be no bigger than a pinpoint of light, but that pinpoint would be so powerful no rocket-assisted take-off would be necessary. . . . Why are you taking off your tunic?"

"It's getting too warm."

"The fire will die down.... What I'm suggesting, in practice, is a taxicab through time. It's self-evident that motion in excess of the speed of light will exceed the flow of time, but the flow of time is in only one direction. Ergo, if I jumped ten minutes within the next five minutes, I'd be where I am now; but if I could jump fifteen minutes, I'd be hauling you up the stairs five minutes ago.

"You'd need no cumbersome life support system in the cab, for at infinite speed you could time your arrival at the place you wish to reach before your oxygen's used up.... Why are you taking off your skirt?"

"It's getting cooler."

"That's an opposite reaction, which reminds me: Newton's Law—for every action an opposite and equal reaction—still holds. You could reduce the weight of the cab until you'd need a power plant with no more energy than a storage battery.

"You see, Helix, that's the beauty of the Haldane Theory from a classical viewpoint. It unifies the Quantum Theory, Newtonian Physics, Einstein's energy theory, Fairweather's Simultaneity—they'll all dance on the grave of Henry VIII, and I'll join in, waltzing to the strains of $LV^2 = (-T)$ Where are you going?"

"Down to the kitchen, to pick up a few recipes from Halapoff."

"I've just presented you with the greatest formula since $E = MV^2$ and you are going down to talk to a cook.... Say, you're wearing nothing but your boots!"

"That's the idea."

A great nonmathematical truth dawned on him. "Come here, girl."

With hand on hip, leaning nonchalantly against the door, she asked, "Are you jealous?"

"Very much so, of a man named Flaxon, the smartest man I've ever met."

"I'll come," she said, "if you'll promise...."

"All right! All right! I won't talk about the Haldane Theory with you any more tonight.... I should have been a gynecologist."

"That's not the promise I want at all," she said, not moving from the door.

He picked up her skirt and tunic and tossed them into a corner. Opening wide his arms in entreaty he said, "Speak."

"Tell me, what is the Haldane 'swizzle-stick' technique?"

He closed his eyes and threw his palm to his forehead in a gesture of despair. "Out of five thousand three hundred and eighty lines of transcript, you pick out that one phrase. Come, Helix, I'll explain its meaning, and I'll explain why I never attempted to demonstrate it to a tender young virgin, I thought, in a crowded city such as San Francisco."

When he opened his eyes, she was standing very close to him, looking down with love, admiration, and repressed eagerness. He put his arms around her to prevent her escaping to Halapoff.

"When I first met you," he said, "I thought your beauty and grace were unearthly, but I was sorely puzzled by your analytical, rational, unfemalish mind. My father warned me you were not of my time and place. My lawyer hinted that yours was a diabolical intelligence in the form of a woman. Now one question regarding a gossipy tidbit, irrelevant and nongermane, has convinced me you're a woman. Gone forever is my hope of a romance with some eternal Lilith."

"Quit shilly-shallying. Out with it, Don. What's this . . ."

"Why does everyone call me Don?"

"That's what I named you, Don Juan."

"Oh, for Byron's romantic hero?"

"Not exactly. I was thinking more of G.B. Shaw."

"Who's he?"

"Oh, he was nineteenth century. You wouldn't know him."

"That's right. I started at the eighteenth and went the other way."

"We're not gathered here to discuss literature. . . ."

There was a rap on the door, and Haldane tossed his nude but booted bride over his shoulder onto the center of the bed, saying, "Keep behind the curtains till I get rid of this stupid bellhop."

"Give me my clothes," she whispered. "That's no bellhop, and you won't be getting rid of him."

"Are you extrasensory as well as extrasensual?" he said, pulling the curtains together.

Vexed by the interruption, he stalked to the door and threw it open.

His caller, a tall, auburn-haired man, spoke hardly above a whisper. "May I come in for a moment, Haldane IV? My name is Fairweather II."

Haldane fell back and caught himself in the manner of a basketball player making a fall-away jump shot. "By all means, sir. I'm honored."

"I hoped to get here before your mate commenced the nuptials, but I had to interview Hargood before I could come up. He tells me you've inadvertently passed the physical competence and bravery tests. I'm proud of you, son.

"You'll pardon my familiarity, but by now you must know that you and I have more in common than most old friends. Hargood was telling me that you've even stumbled onto my Negative Time Theory?"

"$LV^2 = (-T)$?"

"Exactly!" The compliment in Fairweather's smile almost overcame Haldane's disappointment in relinquishing authorship of the Haldane Theory.

"Won't you have a seat, sir? My mate is a little indisposed at the moment."

Fairweather's gray eyes swept the room as he drew up a chair before the fire. As he thanked Haldane for his invitation, he said, "Still wears those boots. . . ." Then he raised his voice to the curtained bed. "Come on out, woman, and pick up your clothes. Your nudity holds no charm for me."

"Sir, it might be a little embarrassing. . . . I'll get them."

"Don't bother, Haldane. I've seen her behind as often as I've seen her face. Her mother is one of my lazier wives, and I was frequently called upon to change her diapers."

"You mean, sir, that you're her father?"

"Don't hold it against me, son. I was old and tired when she came along. Besides, out of eighty-one there's bound to be a bad one now and then."

"Daddy," Helix squealed from behind the curtains, "I wanted to tell him myself."

"Sir, I'm honored to be your son-in-law, and you have a very unusual daughter, but . . ." Out of the corner of his eye he could see Helix scamper from behind the curtains to grab her clothes. "I have grave doubts about myself. I'm the prize pigeon of the universe. I loved the girl, and she tricked me. Your daughter, sir, is a confidence woman. She conned me with honest trifles to betray me in deeper consequence. . . ."

"Honest trifles!" There came a beldame shriek from the corner. "Papa, he's dragged the name of Fairweather through the mud. He stole my virtue. He drove me to ruin. He's the father of my unborn child. Are those trifles?"

Tucking her tunic into her skirt, she was striding toward the fireplace. "Father, this man betrayed me. I had to marry him to make an honest man out of him."

"That wasn't in our agreement, child," Fairweather chided her. "It's customary for a father to approve of his daughter's suitors."

He turned to Haldane. "She wasn't supposed to marry you, but I suppose it's all right since she was in line to be an old maid when she undertook the assignment. . . ."

"Phooey on you, Father," Helix said indignantly. "You know I turned down four hundred and twenty proposals. . . . As for you, Haldane, out of sixty-five thousand possible M–5s on the planet, you were hand-picked by me. If you're a pigeon, you're a very rare bird."

"I can always count on my daughter to do what I want her to do," Fairweather said, "as long as it does not conflict with what she wants to do. She undertook the mission with half an eye out for a specimen such as you; don't say it isn't so, daughter."

"It is, but quit telling my secrets."

Haldane's mind was spinning from the implications of what he had heard, but one implication stuck out in his mind like an Annapurna rising from the Salisbury Plains. "Sir, if she has turned down four hundred and twenty proposals, she must be a very experienced woman."

"Rather," Fairweather nodded, "but she was too selective for a Hellion. Besides, she was only twenty-two when we regressed her back to six for the trip to earth. Counting the twelve years she has relived on earth, she's only thirty-four. Organically, of course, she is only eighteen."

Bluntly, Haldane turned to her and exploded. "And you were questioning me about my experiences! Why, you were playing around when I was still flying kites, and on this planet. Oh, you must have had some laughs at my experienced conduct. . . . Lighting cigarettes from the wrong end. . . . Practicing yoga."

He was genuinely chagrined, and she placed an arm on his shoulder. There was tenderness and compassion in her voice when she said, "Please don't feel inadequate or inferior, darling. We older women put a far greater value on youthful enthusiasm than we do on practiced skills. And nowhere on Hell is there a man who could raise the general average by .08 of one percent."

Mollified by her contriteness, he grinned. "You Hellion."

"But sir," he turned to Fairweather, "how did you get her back to earth?"

"A device for exploiting the capabilities of the negative time formula. It's not a spaceship, really. More a space dinghy. I'm sure you can deduce the type of vehicle we used."

"But how did you fit her into the time pattern, logically?"

"A transcontinental rocket crashed in the South Pacific. Her parents were killed. There were no survivors, unless you account for the child found miraculously floating on a life raft near the scene. . . . We had to wait for an A–7 couple, you see, for Helix is something of a poetess."

"But how did you know that rocket would crash. . . ." He paused. A time taxicab could cruise forward as well as back. "Strike that question, sir."

"Now, young lady, if you'll hug your father's neck and

go sit silently in a corner, you may soon return to your hymeneal rites, if I'm not abusing the term."

After the ceremony of greeting, Helix sat down and Fairweather turned to Haldane. "If I read your syndrome correctly, you would be willing to help us overthrow the Department of Sociology and set free the human spirit on earth."

"Sir, I was formulating independent plans to throw a wrench into their machinery, when your daughter threatened to walk out on me. She had some business in the kitchen."

"Throwing a wrench is of little value unless you know where to throw it," Fairweather said. "There are few periods in history, and those come early, when one man could alter the course of nations. To eliminate the power of the sociologists, we must destroy the seeds of that power, which were planted before the sociologists came into being.

"We needed a theoretical mathematician to make the drop, because hairline adjustments will have to be made during the approach to earth. Coming back is no problem. You merely click the activating switch.

"We had to send Helix to earth to get you because we never get any theoretical mathematicians among the exiles. Those people are so absorbed in their problems that they care nothing about the government; in fact, they aren't even aware that there is a government. Helix was to plant the seeds of deviationism. Your syndrome is a bonus no one expected.

"For the historical period our experts have chosen, you should not have to stay more than eight years on earth, at the most. If it takes longer, you will be embarrassed, because you will not grow older. We have to stabilize your cellular balance to prevent disease. Also, we'll teach you self-hypnosis to control pain and yoga to control bleeding in the event you break a limb or are cut. Naturally, you'll have to be taught to self-administer certain medical aids.

"A homing device in a filling in your tooth will guide you at night or in heavy weather to the escape vehicle, which will transmit constantly from solar power, so you'll be comparatively safe from harm.

"It will take fourteen weeks of intensive training, after your honeymoon is over, to ready you for the drop."

"But, sir, Helix is . . . I want to be with her when the child is born."

"You'll not be gone over three days, her time. The mechanism is programmed to make up the lost time on the return trip."

"Of course," Haldane said. "I can increase V^2."

"Your capsule is very small, and it's designed to resemble a boulder, but it's too heavy to be moved and can't be split open by any device known to that period in history."

"I'll be given background material on the time and place?"

"Intensively. You'll be given sleep-teaching, hypnotic implants, the entire gamut.

"Language will be no problem. We have scholars who speak it on practically every incoming starship.

"Once you've made the drop, you should take no longer to get adjusted than it would take you if you moved from San Francisco to Chicago."

Fairweather paused and looked into the fire. "One problem puzzles me, because I can't answer it for myself, and you and I are alter egos."

He turned, and a quality in his voice commanded Haldane's absolute attention.

"The method of throwing the wrench will be left solely up to you, because you'll be on the spot and will have to evaluate the situation. You'll be given alternate plans of action at the university, and suggested approach methods, but the final solution will be yours.

"There's a possibility that you might have to choose assassination as a method. Is there anything in your experience that leads you to believe that you are capable of committing murder for your principles?"

Haldane remembered the lethal kick which would have ended Whitewater Jones if Hargood had not stopped him.

"I could murder," he said flatly.

"This is highly personal, son, but I ask it from a knowledge of my own personality: do you feel that your love for Helix could hold you to your purpose, despite the blandishments of females who might seek to dissuade you?"

"Sir, I'm on to their tricks. I learned about women from her."

"There's one final question, an important one: is your resolution deterred when I tell you that the language you must learn is Hebrew?"

Inwardly, Haldane whistled.

He had never considered deicide.

Sitting here on another planet, it was easy enough to contemplate. But lining that Figure up in the sights of a crossbow would be a far different matter when the time came to do it.

Oh, hell, he remembered, the crossbow wasn't even invented until He was sixty-five, only five years before He died, He would have to get to Him before He was forty, and that would mean using a knife or a spear.

But it didn't have to be by assassination, he reminded himself.

He was going to make very sure that it wasn't.

He raised his eyes to Fairweather. "The resolution is modified, but it's not deterred."

Suddenly he smiled. "Sir, if I had the training, I'd be ready in three hours for the Israel drop."

"Braggart," Helix said.

"Then that clears up the excuse for my rather unusual call."

He rose, shook hands, bent to kiss Helix, and paused at the door.

"After your honeymoon, drop on over to the university. We've reconstructed a Hebrew village with the gear they used and the food they ate.

"Your instructors will be Pharisaic Jews for the most part, unreconstructed, and they'll be fighting the Battle of Jerusalem all over again. Don't get involved with their political bias, because you'll probably be on the other side.

"They'll call you by your cover name, which will be

Judas, a rather common name for the area at that time, and one that doesn't figure in His annals. The full name, I remember, is Judas Iscariot."

Epilogue: Earth Revisited

HE DETESTED CAMPUS RALLIES WITH THEIR LANK-HAIRED girls and bearded boys. No self-respecting student of mechanical engineering would be seen at one. But he was cutting across campus to the Student Union, and he saw the girl when he had to skirt the edge of the crowd.

She was standing apart from the other listeners, her dark hair flowing back from a high forehead, looking at the speaker with amused contempt in her brown eyes. From her coloring and the soft curves of her body, he figured she was Lebanese.

He recalled the words of a long-dead friend: "In one corporeality, the inscrutable Orient, the lush and perfumed South, the crisp and sparkling North, and the audaciousness of the West. Aye, Hal, the vintage wine of love is quaffed only from Levantine tuns."

Usually William Shakespeare knew what he was talking about, but at just about that time, Hal remembered, Bill had a thing going with a girl from Aleppo. Nevertheless, he stopped beside her, pretended to listen to the speaker, and turned to her. "What's the protest this time."

"Tuition again," she answered. "The speaker's trying to organize a boycott of the university."

"A Roman student named Junius tried that once, and Domitian Flavius had him drawn and quartered in the Forum."

"For all of his effectiveness, this one could be Junius. I hunger to teach these students basic organizing techniques."

"Since you hunger," he said, "and I'm on my way to the cafeteria, I'll treat if you'll teach."

She turned and looked at him more closely. "Are you trying to impress me with your heavy spending?"

"No. I won at gin rummy, last night, and I'm trying to get rid of some loose change."

"Usually I charge more than thirty cents, but I go at bargain rates on Friday."

With few students in the cafeteria line during class period, she had a chance at a leisurely pick of the tarts. Taking a poll of her profile, her skin coloring, and her thin Semitic brow, he came up with the concensus— lovely. And her languid alertness as she haggled within herself over a choice of doughnuts was an expression straight from the bazaars of the Middle East.

"Are you Lebanese?" he asked as they threaded their way to a table.

"No. Greek. My name is Helen Patrouklos."

'Twas not so far south as Aleppo nor so far east as Baghdad, but 'twas enough, 'twould serve.

"Since we're reviving ethnic jokes," she remarked, "are you a Dutchman?"

"No," he said. "I'm a Hebrew, Hal Dane. D-a-n-e."

"That's an unusual name for a Jew."

"It wasn't the original name. My Hebrew name was Iscariot."

"Judas Iscariot, no doubt," she said, selecting a table. "And no doubt you're pulling my leg."

"Would I could experience such delight."

"That's just an expression, silly."

"But pithy and earthy," he said, "I love your modern slang."

"Modern! That one's as old as twenty-three skid-doo."

"I know," he said. "I first heard it from an old love of mine who was interested in such antiquities."

"Where is your old love, now?" Her question was edged with personal concern, and he thought, This girl is smitten with me.

"Lost in the wastes of time," he assured her, "somewhere beyond Arcturus."

"You are a weirdo! . . . May I dunk?"

"Pray do."

She was the first girl he had seen since the dawn of the Christian Era who dunked a doughnut into coffee with charm. "If I may get personal," he said, "I admire your grace of hand and wrist as you sweep into the final movement of the dunk."

She raised her eyebrows and looked at him over the lifted doughnut. "Don't tell me you're a Lit major?"

"No. Mechanical engineering."

"You sound like a poet *cum* historian."

Something about this conversation reminded him of one occurring almost at this place and this time on his first trip around, when he had initially underestimated the power of a woman.

"I was turned against poetry by that ungrateful John Milton," he said, "who painted Satan in such an epic manner that people aren't able to recognize him anymore. He's got too much sense to pose as a Prince of Darkness. For all we know, Satan may be a typical father-in-law with nothing more unusual than a peculiar brand of wit."

"You are a nut, Hal, but I like you."

He could not tell whether she was sincere or pretending, but that distinction would always remain one of the mysteries of life to a male burdened with the honesty of the maladroit.

"What's your major?" he asked.

"Social science."

"I should have guessed. You're always found at rallies."

"Not I," she said. "You don't organize with television publicity, student sit-ins, boycotts. It's not that easy. You form organizations by creeping from mind to mind, convincing as you go."

"Are you organizing something?"

"Yes. An international organization of students to foster world friendship on the young-adult level. In addition to the exchange students on campus, I'm writing to students in England, Russia, Argentina. I have an eager young fellow in Haifa who's burning to organize Israel. But he writes in Hebrew and I write in English. . . . Do you speak Hebrew?"

178

"Fluently," he said, "in several dialects."

"Are you serious, Hal?"

"Absolutely. I also speak Arabic, Greek, Italian, French, German, Spanish, and Russian."

"Say something in Greek," she challenged.

"Pure Athenian or with a Cretan accent?"

"Speak in Athens Greek," she said, "but speak slowly."

He was positive she was bluffing, but he did not speak slowly. He spoke in a conversational tempo, and he spoke the truth: "You are one of the most beautiful girls I have ever seen, and though I know that beauty and virtue are seldom found together, with you it would make no difference. Literally, I could make love to you for one hundred years and not grow tired, if you should last so long."

She dropped her eyes in wonderment and pleased shyness and said, "I saw your lips moving but I couldn't understand a word you said."

So she had understood every word. Well, the truth was the truth.

Suddenly she leaned toward him, speaking intently. "Our movement could use your language talents. No—I'll be more honest with you. I need you. All that I could offer would be my deep appreciation and the satisfaction you would gain from laboring in a cause greater and more enduring than either you or me."

She was waving her hands in the manner of the Greeks —or the Jews—and those hands, her dark eyes, the Semitic cast to her features ripped him with a nostalgia he fought to conceal. Once again he was in old Jerusalem, and the girl across from him was Mary Magdalene. She had the same intensity, driving, persuasive, unselfish, of Mary Magdalene, and she was using almost the same argument that Mary had used when she had persuaded him to turn over his seat to Joshua, now called Jesus, and relinquish passage to their friend on the last starship from earth.

Patterns never changed. The tides of history were sweeping back, and his only earthly love had come again. Mary Magdalene sat before him only slightly changed in form and manner, and her wit and her expressions were those of his only unearthly love, Helix. He bowed his head, pretending to pinch his nose bridge—she even described him as "silly" and "a nut," as Helix did.

When he raised his eyes, Helen was silent, but the pleading continued in her gaze.

"Tell you what, Helen; why don't I drop by your pad tomorrow evening? We can turn over the idea and see what crawls out."

"I'll be in to you," she said, speaking as she wrote her address onto notepaper, "because I like you and I think you could be very valuable to the organization. Your social thinking is probably out of focus because you're an engineer, but engineers are men of action."

"Yes," he agreed, accepting her address. "When it comes to action, we're in the top three per cent, particularly in matters relating to unions between students."

"Oh, I trust a nut," she said, rising, "and I thank you for the treat and the conversation. But I must hurry to Man and Civ. Don't forget Saturday. Come around six, and I'll fix you a bite."

He would remember Saturday, he knew, as he watched her walk from the table with a swaying movement that reminded him of Helix. He had been thinking of Helix more often of late. In a matter of seconds now, her time, she and her dad were going to have the surprise of their lives when the door of the space taxicab opened and the Hebrew Prophet stepped out. Or maybe they wouldn't.

Well, he had had to do it that way; there had been too many questions left dangling between here and out there. As Flaxon had once said, the truth lay in the eye of the beholder, and Haldane had weak eyes. Not that he believed that any deliberate lies had been told; it was just that the truth behaved strangely in the presence of Fairweathers. And Joshua's parables were crystal clear if one took into consideration that crystals bend light, and Haldane IV, alias Judas Iscariot, alias Hal Dane, had never been skilled in spectrum analysis.

For one thing, Haldane wondered if he had sidetracked history or derailed it when he laid the hissop-drugged body of Jesus into the one-seater right after the Crucifixion. Personally, he couldn't lose either way. If he had triggered Armageddon when he launched the starship, then it was oblivion for him and he could use the sleep. That filling in his tooth was giving him a bad time, and he couldn't have it removed. Any dentist would take one look at that receiving set, figure him for a foreign agent, and yell for the F.B.I.

Once the F.B.I. found out he had been a citizen of Georgia for three hundred years, they'd know that Georgia wasn't the one next to Alabama and call in the C.I.A. The C.I.A. would check with Interpol and the International Police would call Istanbul, Damascus, Rome, Paris, London and Moscow (Oh boy! He hoped they never checked Tbilisi and got word from the descendants of Ailya Golovina) and somebody would start figuring that something had gone slightly askew.

He could see the headlines, now, in 48-point Futura bold:

"WANDERING JEW" DISCOVERED ALIVE: ADMITS HE WAS JUDAS ISCARIOT!!!!

Wouldn't the goyim be fried to find that Judas Iscariot was a Christian?

The tooth was making his mind wander.

Helen Patrouklos paused at the entrance to wave good-by to him, and the Wandering Jew waved back. At the precise moment his hand fell to the table-top, a plaintive-voiced cowboy started to sing, "I jest caint bear to say good-by."

If he had engineered the final merger of the ultimate thesis with the ultimate antithesis, then it would be the great Jubilee and nobody would lose, except possibly the professor of economics at Marston Meadows.

The tooth wouldn't be so troublesome if he could pick up a little popular or classical music now and then.

He couldn't lose by joining Helen. If her organization helped bring harmony to this world, then harmony might speed the development of a decent technology. If not, he would still have the pleasure of her company, and he would need all the diversion he could find; at the present rate of scientific progress it would be another two thousand years before he could catch a starship off this cruddy planet.

There was another possibility he dreaded. He might have to tarry until He returned, and that would mean Purgatory if he were doomed to walk the earth, somewhere between the sophomore and junior class, for the next ten thousand years. Life would really be tedious, jest a-settin' . . . just sitting and listening to his tooth play that gosh-derned country and western music *all* the time.